Hitler Burns Detroit

Also by Allan (Dare) Pearce

Paris in April, a novel
*Who Takes This Child? A Parents' Guide to Child
    Protection in Canada*

Hitler Burns Detroit

Allan Dare Pearce

iUniverse LLC
Bloomington

HITLER BURNS DETROIT

iUniverse books may be ordered through booksellers or by contacting:

iUniverse LLC
1663 Liberty Drive
Bloomington, IN 47403
www.iuniverse.com
1-800-Authors (1-800-288-4677)

ISBN: 978-1-4917-1653-3 (sc)
ISBN: 978-1-4917-1654-0 (e)

Library of Congress Control Number: 2013921851

Printed in the United States of America.

iUniverse rev. date: 12/02/2013

For Milly and Clayt

Acknowledgements

I wish to acknowledge the efforts of freelance editor, Marie-Lynn Hammond, who reviewed the manuscript at various stages and provided excellent advice on the content in addition to her always-competent editing efforts.

Do I look crazy? Aiken Day blasts into the bathroom, and the door slaps against the metal stop. He leans, hands on either side of the mirror, and checks his face.

His roommate, Boris, perched on the crapper, pulls the June issue of *Playboy* down from his face and speaks up. "The room ith occupied."

"Do I look crazy? I meet the psychiatrist tomorrow."

"You aren't exactly pretty."

"But I don't look sled-dog psycho?"

"The room ith occupied." Miss June unfolds, the page gracefully falling down to reveal her splendour, and Boris speaks softly, reverently. "Holy thit."

Aiken thinks, *Will the psychiatrist even care what I look like?* He steps back, arms outstretched; he presses, flexing biceps, and does a push-up against the wall. He plunks forehead to mirror, repeats, up and down, and keeps at it for several minutes, until his muscles whine.

His eyes focus. He examines his face once again. *Shit. Shit. Shit. You can't look crazy when you meet the doc for the first time. Shit. Shit. Shit.*

What if the sweats hit me up in a monstrous way? He flicks sweat away from his cheek and rubs fingers together. *Damp! Maybe when I see him the sweat has already dried. Or maybe I splash water on my head, so it seems I come straight from a shower, with a towel draped casually over one shoulder. Mr. Relaxation. That's it: Mr. Goddamn Relaxation.* "Hello, Doc, so nice to finally meet you." *A slow wipe with the towel.* "Just had to clean up a bit for our chat."

"The room ith occupied."

* * *

Aiken whips into the bathroom and places a hand on either side of the mirror again. "Hello, Doctor," he says to the mirror. "I am not crazy." *Not good enough.* "I am not crazy," he repeats, only slower. *Emphasize the* I. "I . . . am not crazy." *Better, but still crazy. Goddamn, the first thing to spill out is that I'm seeing him under court order and not a bonkers situation. The guy seeing the doc before me probably ran down Main Street naked, and the guy behind me probably whipped it out in front of a busload of nuns.* "Only reason I am here, Doc, is that I popped a guy at a civil-rights demonstration." *Shit, that makes me sound racist; like I'm against civil rights and black people. Shit. Shit. Shit.*

"I was mixing it up with a fella, Doc." *Shit. Mixing it up? That makes me sound like Betty Crocker.* "I was fixing to bake you a cake, Doc."

Try the unvarnished truth. "Okay, Doc, a fella with a badge was bothering my wife, and I bounced a stapler off his head."

What's a psychiatrist gonna say to that? Maybe pop some sarcasm at me: "And I suppose, Mr. Day, that you viciously tossed a few paper clips at his partner?" *Or maybe:* "Stealing school supplies when this incident occurred, were you, Mr. Day?" *Or worse:* "Why does a grown man choose a stapler as a weapon of war, Mr. Day? Something symbolic in that, I wonder? What does that stapler actually stand for in your subconscious, Mr. Day? Feeling castrated by organized, modern life, perhaps?"

They always twist it back to castration.

Should I tell him about my fevers? Or about the hallucinations? Shit.

Boris pounds on the bathroom door. "It'th my turn, Aiken. We have to thare."

"In a minute. I am practising crazy." *Or maybe not-crazy. I haven't decided yet.*

Maybe it's best to look crazy when you meet him, so he just shoves a few pills at you and boots you out of his office. I can do crazy. Aiken undoes his fly, reaches inside his pants, and pulls his shirttail through the zipper. He looks into the mirror and sticks his tongue out to the side of his mouth, forcing spittle to dribble down his chin. *Goddamn it, now this* is *crazy.* He looks down. *Oh, man—that sort of looks like a white pecker sticking out down there. What do I tell the doctor when he sees that? What would he twist that into?*

Control the session. That's the trick. You have to give him something offbeat, or he analyzes every ass-pimple to death. So give him something easy to chew on. Hey, Doc, my most favourite day of all time occurred before I was even born. On September 6, 1912, I should have been sitting in Fenway Park watching Smoky Joe Wood piss down the shoulders of Walter Johnson. The greatest pitching duel of all goddamn time, and I wasn't even born. Smoky Joe never held back anything. He threw down smoke. He pissed down smoke. And goddamn Walter Johnson pissed right back at him. But for one or two pitches, either man could have won. They did what real men do. They pissed down as best they could and let the chips fall. They made their own history.

"My turn, Aiken!"

Tell him my least favourite time. Hey, Doc, during the war I busted down in Stalag 8B concentration camp for four years. I don't remember many of those days. The fevers swamped me. Always the fevers. The shitter in Stalag 8B was a 40-holer. I remember that. You shit alone. There might be 39 people beside you, but you shit alone. Some days in the camp you prayed to live; some days you prayed just to die quick. Some days you didn't bother praying, knowing there was no sense to anything.

There was no umpire in Stalag 8B, so we never got to bat. They scored runs against us, but we never got to piss down on anyone. The Jews! It was about the Jews. Who in hell knew it then? You're on the crapper. Look to the left. Look to the right. No Jews in sight. Shit. They would have burned up Hank Greenberg and stopped him from swinging timber just because he was a Hebe. The Hebrew Hammer punched down without a chance to piss back. No sense to it.

Banging on the door. "Hurry up, Aiken!"

Aiken presses fingers to his cheek. *Dry as a bone. Dry as a goddamn bone! Screw it. I'm going with not-crazy.*

12th Street, Detroit

Hot, humid, and bubbling; it's a simmering July night in the Detroit slums. Monroe Johnson touches a finger to his right cheek and drags it along the three-inch scar. He's a thin black army vet of North Africa and Vietnam with no job and nothing to do but cruise the pool halls and jazz joints with all the other Detroit blacks: up and down 12th Street on a Saturday night. Money pokes in his pocket, enough for the occasional cheap shot of hooch in each place but not enough for an old-fashioned drunk-up; so he nurses each shot, dragging it out, listening to the sweet-cooking sounds of Aretha Franklin or some other Motown star. On the streets he sorts through the crowds, ignoring the slicked-down black fellows cruising up and down streets, pimping in their glistening Cadillacs, selling women from their cherished Lincolns, dropping their string out on the streets. In the early hours of the night, Monroe gravitates to the blind pigs, observing late-night gamblers hunting up action in back rooms, crouching and spinning dice or huddling in the second stories of rundown bars, flipping cards. Monroe's pocket money does not stretch for gambling, so he becomes background to the gaming, still hoarding, still nursing every drink. On the street he swings wide of the addicts, festering souls pleading money for one more hit, ready to do crime to raise some coin. Close to the end of his night, he pushes into the blind pig at Clairmount and 12th and wanders into a private party for two returning Vietnam vets who he knows slightly. The party is boisterous but controlled. Monroe is older, more subdued than the rest, and after a decent amount of time, he pushes into the main room and watches gamblers shoot craps on a pool table. The game is the centre of attention. A man pushes by him: broad shoulders, weapon tucked into his waistband at the back. *Undercover cop?* wonders Monroe. Wary of trouble, he slips outside. The blind pig is raided, and 82 people are arrested. Monroe watches the crowd gather, sees the festering, feels the smouldering rage. His finger wanders along his facial scar once more.

* * *

Feisty Paris Day was not involved; she was surveying—contrary to her nature—just surveying. Detroit's 12th Street was blowing apart in rage and Paris Day just surveying; rioting was still just a bubble but escalating even now. Finally it started: the first police car trashed and turned, black men energized; relief washed into her. She made the phone call to the hospital to set it up, paid a man gas money, and that put her across the river into Windsor at the steps of the hospital. People bunched into the hospital elevator: working folks, nurses. White nurses working the midnight shift were trying to stretch their coffee break out. Paris Day edged to the back after pressing the button for the seventh floor, not the eighth, the floor she actually aimed for. The other passengers punched in their own floors. At the seventh floor, the last person exited: a stocky nurse, with flabby arms and girdle-enclosed stomach, she turned and looked back at Paris. Paris shrugged. "Must have been five," Paris said. When the door slid closed, Paris slapped the button for the eighth floor, the psych ward, and rode the elevator up to the top. Off the elevator, a short hallway butted up against security doors. The double doors to the psych ward admitted no one, unless the person showed themselves through the slit window to the Shift Attendant, who could buzz them in.

Paris Day waited outside the unit doors, a slim, handsome woman, wearing Levi's blue jeans and leather coat, with her hair dragged back by a red bandana. The reflections of light danced off her purple skin. She stared out a window. The city of Detroit showed in the distance, and a bright spot flamed up. A lone gunshot sounded a few minutes later.

Inside the psych ward, the Black Janitor swooshed the mop back and forth, working toward the unit doors. At 3 a.m., he called over his shoulder, "I won'ts be long, sir," dipping his head up and down and adding quietly, to himself, "After all, I is the Black Janitor, massa." The Shift Attendant, pulling a double shift, waved a hand and slipped down in his chair, letting the *Free Press* sports section waffle over his face. His eyes closed. The Black Janitor fussed about the doors, swishing the mop back and forth, back and forth. When the Shift Attendant's head nodded, the Black Janitor pulled a finger up and cricked it in and out. A young black woman, wearing a hospital gown, open at the back, and hospital-issued cloth slippers, shuffled into the hallway.

"Move quickly now, Linda," the Black Janitor whispered. Linda rippled toward the unit doors, ass-cheeks bouncing, eyes focused on the sleeping attendant. She slipped out the doors.

Outside the unit doors, Paris Day flicked a finger at Linda. "Come over here," Paris said. She peeled off her leather boots and slid them toward Linda. After a brief silence, they stripped off their outer clothes while facing one another. Paris stripped down to a white satin bra and matching panties, Linda to cotton underpants and no bra over her generous, sagging breasts. Paris stripped off her red bandana and passed it over. She handed over her jeans and coat to Linda and received the hospital gown in return. Linda stared at the expensive underwear. "Just the sort of fancy undies they issue to crazy people," she said.

Paris peeled off the lingerie and Linda pulled down her cotton underpants. They both stood naked now. Paris handed the white garments over, and Linda stuffed herself into them. When done, she offered up the bulky cotton underpants to Paris. Paris shook her head.

"Not so fancy, huh? Suit yourself," Linda said. "Freeze it off, for all I care. Let it drop on the floor without anyone using it, collecting full of dust." Linda balled up the garment and threw it toward the white garbage container resting in the corner. Paris pulled on the hospital gown, wrapped the ties around her waist, and knotted them. "I'm giving up three squares for you," Linda said. "I need some bread."

"You get a free pass out," Paris said.

"You want to skip this whole thing, I could show your husband a few tricks, him being a good-looking white dude who fancies the taste of chocolate." She moved her hands to the overflowing bra, cupping her breasts. "You got anything like these tomatoes to give him?" Paris reached into the fringed-leather shoulder bag at her feet and produced a twenty-dollar bill. Linda pulled herself into the jeans, dragging up the zipper, trying to press the snap together but leaving the jeans open an inch when the snap wouldn't catch. She pulled Paris's blouse over her shoulders and fussed the buttons closed. "I could get more for turning you in," Linda said. "You being a famous civil-rights fugitive, like Stokely Carmichael, and all."

Paris jabbed a finger hard into the woman's chest. She slipped unconsciously into black dialect. "Maybe you shut your face and move on, girl." A grimace played across Linda's face. She crumpled the bill into a pocket and plodded down the hall toward the elevator. Paris pulled plain cotton underpants from her bag and drew them on, then snapped the hospital gown back down in place. She slipped inside the unit, nodded to the Black Janitor, and padded down the hall in the rag slippers, gliding through the third door as the Black Janitor pointed to it. Inside the room, the pretty blonde girl, Honey, the only rapid-cycling manic-depressive on the unit, as well as the only one claiming to be a Marxist-Leninist, bounced open an eye without lifting her head from the pillow. "Can't sleep, Linda?" she said.

Paris stuffed her bag under the second bed. "Call me Paris," she said, plopping down on the bed. "All my friends do."

"Paris, the city of hope," Honey said. She giggled but a few minutes later started sobbing into her pillow and fell asleep. A soft snore dropped out of the blonde, shushing across the room. The wind from the girl's nostrils bounced off the pillow and puffed a ribbon of blonde hair up and down.

"Not *hope*, dearie—*light*," Paris said. "Any hope in the Motor Cities is fading."

* * *

In a different part of the psych ward, Aiken Day faced his own smouldering threat. Usually the fevers punched him into troubled sleep, but on occasion they knocked him down lower, into the barren, almost bottomless, sphere of shadows, spooks, and spirits. On this night while Detroit simmered, the meds faded, abandoning him, but he rallied and struggled as the sheets wrapped about his torso, waking him. *Jesus H. Christ, a goddamn inferno plucks at my brain.* He staggered from his bed and paced the room. The fever receded but then bounced back; he paced 12 steps down the room and 12 back. The fever kicked up full bore, and he swooned, stumbled, and caught himself; he shook his head and ran fingers through dark, tousled, damp hair. "Give me a goddamn break," he said. *I'm on fire and back in the war.* Outside, a muffled gunshot sounded. *Shooting people in Detroit?* The sweats increased.

Aiken remembered gunshots and the heat of fire from the war. *Fire bombs—incendiaries—blasted cities apart, set people on fire: Coventry, Dresden, Berlin, and Leningrad, all in flames; Hiroshima and Nagasaki vaporized in a goddamn instant.*

Aiken's regiment, the Essex Scottish, local fellas from Windsor and Essex County with a few Detroit Yanks tossed in, had landed on the beach at Dieppe, in France; 553 men had battled ashore under heavy fire, chaps he'd hunted with, told jokes to, lied to, pissed beside, and drank with; they'd been boyhood chums. Just 52 had returned to England the following day, the rest dead, splat on the beach, maybe rolling with the surf, or like Aiken Day, stuffed into a concentration camp for the rest of the war. In Stalag 8B, he'd paced 12 feet down and 12 feet back during those four godforsaken years, fevers slapping at his soul, brain infernos, and he'd learned about the oven fires. Hitler had killed the retarded Germans first, burned 10,000 crazies even before starting on the Jews, but after that it had been the Jews. They'd incinerated Jews to the very end of the war.

A faint explosion registered with him. *Detroit again. What shit is seeping out of the ghetto tonight?*

Across the room, a sleeping Boris snorted. *Christ, the kid is snoring again; never heard such grisly sounds. Maybe it's all the drugs he used to do. Or maybe it's caused by the lisp. Damn shame that people assume he's queer.* Another snort slipped out. *At least there's a minute of silence between each one. Just enough time to stop me from crossing the room and throttling him. I wonder if he lisps in his dreams.*

Aiken left the room and shuffled down the hall, edging toward the lounge, right arm outstretched, dancing his fingers along the wall to keep himself from weaving, and after a few steps he steadied. *And the goddamn sweats fade slowly, ever so slowly, beginning to leave me. They'll take a brief vacation before the next damn attack.*

Aiken discovered the Fat Man in the lounge. "Morning, Mr. Day," the Fat Man said. "Whom the gods would destroy, they first make mad. They should keep the wretched kitchen open at night." The Fat Man was sprawled across the couch, knees wide apart. Aiken shook his head. *Stained grey underpants beneath a plaid flannel housecoat; munching from an extra-large bag of greasy potato chips and slurping Orange Crush soda from the can. One asks the obvious question: "Is an invitation to dine at Buckingham Palace in the works? Elegance in the psych ward . . . shall I uncork the Bordeaux, sir?"*

Aiken leaned against the doorway, shoulders racking up most of the space. "Maybe they should set you up with a conveyor belt," he said. "Or make a bed for you in the kitchen."

"Children and fools tell the truth, Mr. Day. And you are definitely not a child."

They waited together in silence for a few minutes, until the Fat Man took note of the sweat on Aiken's face. "Somebody thrust your head into a toilet?" the Fat Man said.

"This is nothing," Aiken said, wiping some sweat from his cheeks. "I sweat like this all the time. I sweat worse than this just deciding what socks to put on."

The Fat Man nodded, producing a slurping sound with the pop can. "Do I care?" the Fat Man asked. "Do I really give a fig? Not a whit for you, Mr. Day."

Aiken's ears registered the sound of distant gunshots, and he shuffled to the windows and glanced down on the scene, peering down at the city of Windsor, his eyes rolling across Windsor streets to the Detroit River and then over the river to the American side, stopping at Detroit. Flames shot up from a building in Detroit. *Bigger than a house. Multiple houses, or maybe some slimeball apartment building.*

The Fat Man slouched up and pressed against the window, watching Detroit. He jerked away suddenly, dropped his pop can, and ran out into the main hall of the unit, where he screamed, "They're putting Detroit to the torch! The coons are burning Detroit!" He caught his breath, leaned back against the wall, and yelled again. "Wake up! The niggers are burning Detroit!"

As Aiken watched, the Fat Man's screams roused patients from sleep, and those people pulled others awake; the rooms in the ward emptied, and patients struggled, throwing off the last traces of their meds. They shifted down hallways, slippers flapping on marble floors, nudging toward the lounge, anxious. They gathered about the Fat Man, who collected them in, gesturing and prodding them through the double doors, toward the windows of the lounge; they pressed and huddled together out of nervousness.

Aiken was startled to spot his own wife among the patients straggling in. He saw the familiar smile break across her face, a scrappy smile that spread, crackling across her coal-black features. She clicked the room's light switch off, and suddenly the burning scene in Detroit leaped out in vivid detail, popping into everyone's focus: flames across the river, flames in Detroit.

The blonde girl, Honey, said, "We're all gonna die." Now a creeping, creepy silence took over; no one turned a face away from Detroit.

Aiken backed up, pushing to a place beside Paris. Voice low, he asked, "What are you doing here? The police are hunting for you."

"Call me Linda," Paris said. "All my friends do."

Aiken dabbed his fingers against his temple once more, a deliberate, measured gesture; he detected fingers slippery to the touch, but just slippery, not dripping wet, a good sign most days. "You look nothing like Linda," he said.

"Especially the boobs. That's what you were thinking."

"What?"

"Only you can see me, cupcake, but you're in love. The rest of these people can't tell one black person from another. I'm invisible to them."

"They're offering a money reward for you," Aiken said.

"Yeah," Paris said, "but the reward for Stokely is much higher. It's a damn sexist world."

"Why are you here?" Aiken said.

"I need you to come with me. Stuff's happening in Detroit, and we need to be there."

"Who will care for the kids?"

"My dad can watch my two kids for a while longer," Paris said.

"*Our* kids, Paris," Aiken said. "They're *our* kids, not *your* kids."

"Yeah, our kids," Paris said. "You made them that. But they are black, like me, and they just ain't gonna make it in this white world. They are too damn dark."

To mollify her, he said, "The meds help. I'll be off the eighth floor and home soon."

Honey wobbled over and stood beside them. She sobbed. "Look at Detroit, Linda." She swung a finger up and wiped at her blonde bangs. "This will never end." Paris turned away from her and hunched in closer to Aiken.

"I need to stay here for now," Aiken said. "I need a good assessment from the psychiatrist, and I need to go home, park my butt down on Victoria Avenue, and get back to teaching."

"Sure," Paris said, "and don't forget drinking goddamn imported beer all day long and grilling steaks, oblivious to the world." Other conversations in the lounge fell away. "Aiken," Paris said, "you spent four years in a concentration camp. They won't do anything to you for smacking someone at a civil-rights demonstration. So leave with me, now."

Aiken did not reply.

"In this city," Paris said, "with all the Dieppe vets, you'd have to shoot the Queen Mother in the ass to get actual jail time. You know that's true."

Honey giggled. "Shoot the Queen Mother in the ass," she repeated.

Aiken bent over to whisper. "Your roommate," he said, "seems a complete nutcase."

"It's the goddamn psych ward," Paris said. "Maybe you meant to check in at the Holiday Inn?"

The Fat Man slid in beside Aiken. "I forgot you married dusky," he said. "I got no problem with coloureds of any kind, Mr. Day. I meant nothing. Tastes differ. I just used the wrong words. I'm friends with Linda. Just ask her."

Paris smiled, nodding. "Yeah, friendly—he's just an ordinary guy."

Aiken slapped the Fat Man in the chest, a rabbit punch, but hard-driven and the Fat Man staggered back one step. "I married dusky," said Aiken. "I understand the consequences. You didn't mean nothing." The Fat Man melted away a few steps in the face of Aiken's anger. Aiken calmed down, speaking quietly to himself. "But it ain't just a question of terminology, pal."

The pencil-thin Minister, the only person on the unit with sex charges pending, paced back and forth until he stopped beside Aiken. "They will come for us," the Minister said, making a cross over his heart. "They will certainly come for us."

The Fat Man laughed. "Oh yeah," he said, "absolutely. They'll want to kill the crazies first. Big fish eat little fish—always have, always will."

Honey laughed at that, bending over in mirth, hooting. "Big fish," she said. "Oh, that's so funny."

"Right." Aiken spoke quietly once more. "Why kill the crazies? What in hell was Hitler thinking?"

Paris ran a finger down Aiken's damp cheek. "Soak up the sweat," she said. "You need to get off the psych ward."

"We should go home together. We've earned the good life."

"You are not listening to me," Paris said. "Our jet-black daughter has outgrown and thrown out all of her dolls, except one. Care to guess which one?"

"What?"

"The white one," Paris said. "She still keeps the white one, still hugs her white doll every night. But she tossed all the black ones into the garbage."

"And?" Aiken said.

"And, I'm not sitting anything out," she said. "And I'm not being tossed into the garbage."

"The kids need you at home."

"I'm like that extra-special present at Christmas," Paris said. "Or maybe like a favourite aunt, come to visit, but it's you they actually need every day. They would die without you, Aiken."

"Come home."

"You stole their hearts," Paris said. "While I was doing Alabama sit-ins, and marching in Washington, and licking stamps for JFK, you stole their hearts. You play big-guy stuff, baseball and basketball, with Adam, and you steal my daughter's love every single day. I can't change that."

"Now is when they need you." Aiken said. "Now, while they're still kids."

"I do this for them. I do it instead of barbecuing my life away on Victoria Avenue."

"Well, it's true," he said. "I'm gonna live on Victoria Avenue, sucking down green bottles of beer. I'm gonna live with our two kids, and you should be there too. Even if you have to fake it for their sake."

"Yeah, our kids," Paris said. A tear formed, and she twisted her head about so that he couldn't see. After a few seconds, she turned back to him. "My kids need me on the barricades, not somewhere faking it up." She started away but then turned back. "Call me Linda," she said.

After a short silence, Aiken said, "Linda it is."

12th Street, Detroit

Monroe possesses the patience drilled into him by the military. He wipes his fingers across the scar that decorates his cheek. He picks his spot on the street, beside a phone booth, where his back presses against a brick wall. He analyses the street scene before him: people are agitated, more agitated than usual. He knows 12th Street to be the most densely populated area in the country, a dilapidated, run-down, rat-infested area with over 20,000 people per square mile; he knows that white police officers refer to 12th Street as "Niggerland Central." In the early hours of Monday morning, he watches the unrest spread slowly, as people gather in the streets, a few at a time and then more, hearing rumours of police abuse. The scar on his cheek tingles. The gathering in front of him spreads and surges. One man tosses a brick at a police car; then more join in, heaving more bricks at any passing squad car. Police arrest more blacks. Toward morning, Monroe learns of the police commander's decision: recall all police vehicles from the area. It may be too late, Monroe thinks.

He sucks in the crowd, swelled now to several hundred; bricks are pounded through store windows. He watches limited looting begin. He watches occasional buildings flame. Are we stealing dry goods or rebelling against whitey? he wonders.

The crowd moves away from the blind pig and sloshes down 12th Street. Monroe follows, still the observer. More and more people leave their homes to join in; the crowd of brown and black faces travels down 12th Street, exploding in size, rage smouldering.

Monday, July 24, 1967
The Psych Ward of Windsor Hospital

At 7 a.m., Aiken's daughter, Sarah, visited him before she went to school. The unit forbade morning visits, but the Black Janitor checked to confirm that the Shift Attendant was occupied elsewhere and unlocked the door for her. Sarah hugged the man and slipped unnoticed down the hall into Aiken's room. She found him still in his pajamas and housecoat.

She wears a school outfit; the blouse with wide white lace wrapping around the collar that emphasizes the blackness of her face. I love that outfit; I love that darkness, maybe even dote on the darkness. What else do you need in life if you have a daughter who beams up at you?

Sarah smiled at him with glistening white teeth, climbed into his lap, and put an arm around his neck, placing her lips next to his ear. "Black people," Sarah whispered. "Negroes started the fires in Detroit."

"Negroes?" he said, running a finger across her cheek. Her eyes fixed on him.

She nodded. "Are you safe here?" she said.

She needs the right answer here. "Yes, I'm safe," he said. "And you?"

"I'm so afraid, Daddy," she said.

"Grandpa Mayhem will take you and your brother to stay at his home in Chatham, away from Detroit and Windsor for a few days. It'll be safer."

"But you could come with us."

"I'll be safe here in the hospital." Aiken swept her up in his arms and kissed her; his forehead was dry as a bone. She smiled at him then and touched his face, fingers dancing along his cheek. Aiken thought: *She has her answer. Not exactly the one she wanted, but she's satisfied with it, comforted for now.*

* * *

At 10 a.m., Aiken sat down in the wooden chair inside the office on the eighth floor, an office of spartan simplicity, airless and windowless. Dr. Sam acknowledged his presence with a nod of the head, not looking up from his notes as he scribbled away. He sported a mop-like twist of red hair and wore a crisp white lab coat; a bright red tie poked out at the collar. Dr. Sam tugged unconsciously at the tie's knot so as to loosen it but quickly gave up, leaving it in place.

"You know, I probably don't need to be here," Aiken said.

Dr. Sam glanced up. "I hear that quite often," he said. He went back to reading the file. "I see that your wife is Negro and wanted by the authorities. What can you tell me about that?"

"Yes, she's a black woman. That's what we call them now." *Very, very black.*

"There is a rumour she's been seen near the hospital," Dr. Sam said.

"Probably someone else," Aiken said. "Maybe someone who looks like her." *Maybe Sonny Liston.*

"Tell me, Mr. Day," Dr. Sam said. "What did you like to do as a child?"

"Baseball and chores," Aiken said. Aiken thought about his youth. *Sweaty summer days in green-fenced ballparks; pick-up games by the hundreds, maybe thousands; diving on red clay infields, chasing down ground balls; waiting to bat, ass plonked on rough wooden benches; smacking a hard line drive; kick-sliding into home plate.* He decided to contribute more. "I actually grew up on baseball," he said. "Mayhem Chase taught me baseball, inside and out."

"Who?"

"My father-in-law."

"Your wife's father?" Dr. Sam said.

"Yes."

"So, this Chase fellow," Dr. Sam said, "is a Negro person."

"A big-sized black man," Aiken said. "And if God had given me Mayhem Chase's shoulders and his heavy-duty right arm, there would be a chocolate bar named after me today, guaranteed."

"Excuse me," Dr. Sam said. "You want some trite candy sweet named after you?"

Aiken said nothing. Dr. Sam laughed out loud. "Ha! On sale here: the Aiken Day Nutbar." He chopped the laughter off, abruptly. "Sorry, a somewhat unprofessional outburst, Mr. Day. That was uncalled for."

Aiken nodded. *Nutbar? Surely preferable to being an asshole.*

"Tell me about your war, Mr. Day," Dr. Sam said.

It's getting hot in here. Shit. "Well, in Stalag 8B they divided us by tribes, much like Detroit these days. You got your coloureds here, your whites here, and your Polacks over there in Hamtramck."

"What?" Dr. Sam said. "Tribes in the prison camp?"

"The Polish tribe here, your Russian tribe in this compound, the British tribe here, and a Canadian tribe, but no Jewish tribe."

"What are we talking about?" Dr. Sam said.

"The Jews were somewhere else. Somewhere worse."

"Really off topic," Dr. Sam said.

"What tribe would they put my wife and kids in?" Aiken said. "The Krauts didn't have no purple compound."

"What?"

My guess: Paris and my kids would go with the Jews, shovelled-into-the-oven compound.

"It's over, Mr. Day," Dr. Sam said.

"Is it?" The sweats eased.

"A few rather obvious observations for you," Dr. Sam said. "Preliminary, of course."

"Sure," Aiken said. "Shoot."

"You apparently live with a Negro wife," Dr. Sam said. He looked up from his notes. "Sorry, a black wife and two black children."

Dr. Sam waited, reflecting.

You get paid for this? "Yes, I do live with black people." *But I've had all my shots. Been fully inoculated, completely eliminating any urge to buy a Cadillac, pimp women, and live in the ghetto.*

The overhead pipes clanged.

"A traditional team sport like baseball," Dr. Sam said, "with uniforms and rules, telegraphs things about a person. Uniforms, Mr. Day. And you joined the Essex Scottish Regiment during the war?"

"Yes." *Next time I'll join up with hippies, wear bell bottoms and beads when I hit the beach. Maybe it'll turn out better.*

"What are your feelings about the civil-rights movement?" Dr. Sam said. "You have two black kids."

Feelings? "Sure. Anyone hurts my family, I slap them down. A man does for family. That's one of the rules I got from my pa. His rules for being a man." *One of the few rules that didn't involve sex or whiskey.*

Dr. Sam made another notation. "Therapy would address this sort of stuff," he said.

"Therapy?"

"To put therapy in a Canadian context," Dr. Sam said and he snickered, "therapy is like having a third elbow in a hockey game. Think of it. A third elbow, Mr. Day."

"Sure."

"We would expose your repressed thoughts and send them to your conscious level."

Holy shit. Beneath crazy, another level of crazy.

Dr. Sam lowered his voice. "Therapy is subject to the good graces of the Administrator, of course."

"The Administrator?" Aiken said.

"Yes, the bitchy government person who sends me memos about your wife."

Dr. Sam put a hand on the lapel of his lab coat and flicked his finger at the collar. "He makes us wear these stupid white coats, with neckties. A damn uniform." Dr. Sam stood and placed his notes in a folder, organizing them briefly, pushing the pages about until they were perfectly aligned. He leaned against the desk.

"So, I get a few more meds," Aiken said.

"Many people on the unit can't be helped," Dr. Sam said. "They just want the drugs. No real effort to engage in proper therapy."

"Repression?"

"Exactly," Dr. Sam said.

Aiken shifted his position, reached down, and scratched his crotch to relieve an itch. When the itch felt better, he smiled briefly.

Dr. Sam caught note of the smile and closed up Aiken's folder. "Good sessions have that effect, Mr. Day. They make you feel better." He pulled a prescription pad, scribbled on it, and passed the slip over to Aiken. He nodded over Aiken's head, signalling for the next patient in line to enter. Aiken rose and ducked out the door, clutching the slip of paper in his hand. As he left the office, Dr. Sam called after him. "A third elbow, Mr. Day."

The next person through Dr. Sam's door, a thin woman with spectacles pushed back against graying hair, pushed in without knocking.

"Another memo from the Administrator?" Dr. Sam said.

"No more staff for the Psych Ward. Just pump more meds into the crazies."

"He actually called them 'crazies?'"

"He said to wire a few up to that electro-shock machine and push them back on the street."

"But *crazies*?"

*　　*　　*

At 8:30 a.m., Monroe fades back from 12th Street, watching black clergy meet at Grace Episcopal Church.

He hunches into the rear of the church, back against the rear wall. Concerns are expressed: lives will be lost if the police intervene in great force. The leaders disperse to the riot areas, seeking to calm people down. Monroe thinks they are a generation too old and a generation too late. Their efforts fail. By 10 a.m., more than 3,000 black people mob back and forth on 12th Street, from Clairmount to West Grand; the area is blocked off at each end by police barricades. The rioters are looting, stealing jewelry, food, guns, and TVs—whatever they find. Monroe observes police officers bantering with the looters, trying to keep tensions at bay; a party atmosphere reigns. Over the next few hours, confused reports flow into police headquarters: things are under control; things are out of control. Monroe hears the white mayor of Detroit advising reporters that things are definitely under control. Reporters laugh and correct him. Monroe listens as the mayor retracts his statement. The riot area grows. Monroe touches his scar, thinks the itching maybe means it is inflamed.

* * *

During morning visiting hours, Aiken's son, Adam, a tall, strapping boot-black teenager, arrived on the unit and guided Aiken out of the lounge, large hands on Aiken's elbow, easing him toward his room. *You're big, like Mayhem, with shoulders to carry the world.* "Somehow you make the room hunch down," said Aiken. Inside the room, Adam began to pace, then pulled the chair up, perched on the edge of the seat, and fidgeted with the buttons on his shirt for a few minutes. A gunshot sounded in the distance, and Adam swung the drapes back from the window. Black rivulets of smoke streamed over Detroit. He swung the drapes shut.

"What's going on with you?" Aiken said.

No reply.

"Nervous about the riot?" Aiken said.

"No, it's in Detroit."

So it's woman trouble. "Girlfriend trouble?" Aiken said.

A few seconds later, Adam rose and began to pace again. He stopped. "Rachael can't date a nigger," he said.

"What happened, exactly?" Aiken said.

"Her father says she's too young to date."

"Grade 11 may be a bit early."

"Rachael dated in Grade 10," Adam said, "and he never objected. So really, Rachael can't date *me*. She's too young to date me and only me."

"Damn."

"Too young to date a nigger," Adam said.

"Adam."

"So, Pops," Adam said, "how old does a girl have to be to date a nigger? Twenty-one? Forty-two? How old? How about ten thousand and two? How old, Pops?"

"Did you talk to your mom about this stuff?" Aiken said.

Adam stopped pacing, "Mom?" he said. "Why? So she could plan a sit-in at their synagogue or whip up some flashy petition?"

"Your mom knows about this stuff, and she cares about you."

"I thought I finally had a steady girlfriend," Adam said. "I can't stop thinking about this stuff. Gimme some guy advice, Pops. Something from your pa."

"Don't use your brain so much."

"We had the don't-get-anyone-pregnant talk," Adam said, "a few years back, so something more. This stuff is driving me crazy."

"My pa maintained that there are three important parts to a man. You got the heart, the brain, and the python." *What he actually said was a man's only goal in life was to drink whisky and screw, but I punched it up after I fell in love with your mom.*

"The *python*?" Adam said.

"You have to find a proper balance between these three things," Aiken said. "That's a man's primary job in life. Don't use your brain on this racism stuff. It'll just drive you crazy. Figure out how to sink a 25-foot jump shot, when the game is tied in the final seconds."

"Python?"

"Put your brain in neutral until you meet someone else," Aiken said. "Someone new."

"Rachel was fun. We laughed our asses off." Adam noticed the sweat on his pa's forehead. He reached for the hand towel on the night stand and passed it over to Aiken, who wiped the sweat away. "You're sweating again, Pops," Adam said. "When do you see the doc?"

"You know, soon."

"Good," Adam said, "he'll fix you up with some pills."

"Give your brain a rest."

"Right, Pops. I'll rest the brain and work on the jump shot."

*   *   *

Aiken turned his prescription in at the nursing station, and the nurse on duty glanced at it. Behind and over her shoulder, the window displayed a sky with billows of dark smoke pluming upward. The head nurse squinted, but after a few seconds she shrugged. "What does the damn thing say?" she said.

Aiken plucked the slip from her hand and tried to decipher the scribbles. "I can't make it out," he said. "It's just chicken-shit scratches. What do I do?"

"Don't fret," the head nurse said. "Medicine in here is pretty much all the same stuff. It's all just stuff to quiet down the brain. Just line up for nighttime meds and grab whatever they give you. We run a relaxed ship here. Why add stress to patients?" Then she whispered, "Why make them any crazier than they are? So don't you fret now, sweetie." She patted Aiken's hand.

Right! Take a pill, any pill, and no fretting on the psych ward. Make a note, Detroit. Take a pill, any pill, and no fretting.

In the lounge on the psych ward, shuttered drapes blanked out the flues of smoke in the Michigan skies. The sound from the unit TV, dialed up as it was, muffled out all but the loudest riot noises. The patients gathered around the TV, sitting in a half circle, each person perched in his or her regular chair, each person mesmerized by a movie that starred Bing Crosby as a hip Catholic priest putting off the established types and solving all problems.

"I just adore Bing Crosby," Honey said to no one in particular. Heads nodded.

Aiken slipped into his own place at the back of the room and leaned against the wall. Paris joined him a few minutes later, standing beside him, leaning in close so that they touched. *She smells of lilac.* "It's Bing goddamn Crosby," said Paris, quietly. "I might just puke on your slippers."

"Thank you," Aiken said. "I never knew his middle name. But give it a rest."

"So much bullshit," Paris said. "Nothing racist about a white problem solver in a pure white world. It works. It truly works."

"You're threatened by Bing Crosby? It's not like he scrubs out toilets, stealing quality black jobs."

"Shut up."

All eyes were riveted to the TV screen. "Paris," Aiken said, "a guy called the Administrator is in charge around here, and they suspect you may be in the hospital. Get out of here while you can."

"Call me Linda," Paris said. "My disguise is perfect, absolutely perfect. I am like wallpaper. If I yanked a pair of trousers on and scrabbled away at my crotch, I could pass for the Black Janitor."

"Except for the boobs," Aiken said.

"Still thinking about Linda?"

The patients watched the movie in silence, totally absorbed with Bing, the pure white problem-solving priest. Only during the commercials did people comment, and the comments revolved around the desirability of having Bing at everyone's church to solve all problems. How wonderful that would be. Everyone agreed. "Puke city," Paris said to Aiken.

The movie resumed after a commercial, but then it suddenly cut out, and the screen switched to the local studio-based newscaster, garbed in dark business suit and bland tie, speaking in serious, weighty tones. "This is Ernest Chapwick at the Channel Two Newsroom. We apologize for interrupting our regularly scheduled program, but the riot in Detroit has not been contained, although at present it remains confined to the northwest part of the city." The scene switched to live shots of 12th Street in Detroit. On the screen, black men raced about breaking windows, looting buildings, and dragging out stolen store merchandise.

"We should be there," Paris said to Aiken.

"Sure, I could use a new toaster. Maybe even pick up a blender."

"Shut up."

The patients in the psych ward remained seated, captivated by the scenes of riot. A reporter at the scene, wearing a dress shirt rolled up at the sleeves, open at the neck with no tie, jammed his face into the microphone and said, "People expect the mobilization of the Michigan National Guard shortly and hope this will stop the looting and burning that we now see in this part of the city." The camera scanned the looters once more and then spun back to the reporter. "This is Frank Morgan, live from 12th Street in Detroit, where rioting and looting continue."

The scene switched back to the Channel 2 newsroom, and the anchorman spoke. "The mayor expects the riot situation to be settled shortly," he said. "But he does recommend that people avoid this part of city for the next hour or so. There is no word yet as to whether the Tigers' scheduled game will be cancelled, but the mayor's office is checking on this and will issue a special emergency bulletin addressed to all Detroit Tiger fans." He twisted his body a few degrees, and the camera closed in on him. "The Tigers will need to pull up their socks if they want to finish in the pennant race this year. Thank you, and now back to our regularly scheduled program."

Paris marched to the front of the room and swung about to face everyone, blocking the TV screen with her body. People gasped. She turned abruptly and switched the set off. Bing disappeared. Murmurs sounded from the patients immediately.

"Put that TV back on," the Minister said. "We have rights."

"Honey catches more flies than vinegar," the Fat Man said. "Step aside, out of the way."

Honey turned to face the Fat Man. "Who? What?" she said.

Gradually, one by one the patients stood up, gathering moral strength from those already standing, and all edged slowly toward Paris Day and the TV.

Paris stands her ground. Fearless! That's my wife.

"Detroit is burning," Paris said, "but the people on that screen are not the only problem."

"Well, believe it or not," the Fat Man said, "just who in hell do you see stealing those toasters, Linda? Or maybe you think the Pope is behind it? Or maybe you figure Elvis engineered this riot?"

Aiken pushed through the group until he stood at Paris's side. He raised his voice. "Everybody, stop right now and just relax." *Christ: bring out more meds; a stinking truckload of pills. Send them down to the psych ward on a conveyor belt.* People stopped moving toward Paris, but no one actually backed up. *So we have ourselves a Mexican standoff.*

"Wait a minute," Honey said, coming to stand on the other side of Paris, draping an arm around her, beginning to cry. "Oh Linda," she said, trying to stifle her sobbing. Tension in the room eased. "I remember downtown Detroit," she said. "I remember Hudson's Department Store at Christmas time. Remember, Linda. Remember how lovely it was, the Christmas tree, the lights, the decorations?" *Good move, Blondie. Tension flies out the window when crazy flies in.*

Aiken's roommate spoke up, "Yeth, yeth; I remember." *Yeth, yeth, yeth. Boris yethes his ass off, and the battlefield permanently shifts.*

"Hudson's?" Paris said. "Yeah, damn pretty, especially to white people, all of whom expected a pure white Christmas as a matter of right—the sort of Christmas established by Queen Victoria and exported to her white colonies. I do recall a white Christmas in Windsor and Detroit that began and ended with shopping at Hudson's, the true white department store."

Honey cried softly. "Oh, they sold beautiful undies, silk undies fit for a Hollywood actress. Myrna Loy once shopped there." She began to laugh, "God, how I miss those undies." She pulled up her underwear, letting everyone see the top inch of the plain white cotton ones that she wore now. "Mom and I would walk up Woodward Avenue," she said, "until we had shopped all the stores. We would push our shopping bags into a cab and lie to the customs officer at the border to finish off the day." She giggled. "What brilliant lies we lied: 'Oh no, nothing to declare, Mr. Customs Officer.'" People relaxed, smiling with Honey. "Oh, we were wicked—wicked!" she said. "We were as wicked as Errol Flynn ever was."

"Well, I remember visiting dumpy clapboard houses on John R Street, with my father," Paris said, "delivering grocery parcels so those folk had something to eat on Christmas day, something to feed to their kids."

"Not my cup of tea," the Minister said. "I never did food to the poor. Too depressing by far."

"A true humanitarian," Paris said.

"Humph," the Minister said. He aimed his next comment at Aiken. "Did you never go down Brush

Street in Detroit," he said, "and see how those coloured people live?"

Paris spoke up, not yelling, but close to it. "Brush Street is where the black prostitutes work, selling themselves for food." The Minister didn't reply but turned and moved off. Paris called to his back, "Do you need your lawyer present before you answer?"

People shuffled away, sensing Paris's anger, and a few left the lounge to seek the comfort of their rooms. Honey put her arm through Paris's arm. "Well, I never worked at Hudson's, but the store was so nice at Christmas. Did you never want to be a shopgirl there?"

"Coloured girls could not work at Hudson's," Paris said, "unless they were paper-bag brown or lighter."

"Oh, that's awful," Honey said. She began to weep.

Paris turned to Aiken, seeking to speak to him and taking his hands in hers, but he suddenly realized what she was about to say and interrupted her. "I'm staying here for now," Aiken said. "But you don't have to save the world today."

"So tell me, Aiken Day," Paris said. "Exactly what would I say to all those whores working on Brush Street?"

"So, another goddamn crusade begins," he said. Paris flicked her head in irritation and left the room.

Aiken bent over, clicked the TV set on, and when the images of the riot bounced about the screen, he switched the channel. The screen suddenly lit up, showing Amos and Andy arguing about something. The laugh track sounded.

"I've seen this episode," the Fat Man said. "It's good. It's priceless."

People resumed their places. The Minister laughed. "Those coloured people are so funny," he said. Aiken smiled. *Crazy settles in for a quiet afternoon of intellectual theatre.*

* * *

Smoke spirals twist up from a one-mile area above 12th Street, still spreading. Monroe snuffs out a cigarette out and approaches a firefighter who is resting, butt perched on porch steps. "Long way from home," Monroe says, pointing to the uniform patch.

"Over from Windsor," the man says. "Ninety-five of us volunteered and crossed the border. Just helping out. Some of the Michigan fire companies are sitting this out because of insurance problems." He glances at the flames in nearby buildings. "The fires will turn into firestorms if we don't get control soon."

"Just what Detroit needs," Monroe says. His eyes glance across the street, to and fro. A building half a block away blows out. "We are losing," the fireman says. Monroe nods. *Or we're already lost*, he thinks.

*   *   *

Paris came to dinner late, selected a seat apart from the others, placed her dinner tray down on the table, and said a brief blessing before starting on her meal. The dining room drapes remained closed tight during the dinner hour, but toward the end of the meal a kitchen worker pulled them back. As the patients finished their meals, they lingered in the dining room in a lighthearted mood. The Shift Attendant joined them with his coffee, prepared to hold court and "blaze away at the crazies," as he sometimes put it to friends.

"Are they are murdering whiteth in Detroit?" Boris asked.

The Shift Attendant said, "My opinion only: they're just trying to pith you off." People smiled. Paris pushed her tray away.

Honey suddenly banged a knee with her fist, giggling hysterically. "Pith you off," she said, "God, that's so damn funny—pith you off," She started to weep, and anxiety on the floor increased. People once again took note of the smoke plumes over Detroit.

"If the Canadian army reacts quickly," the Minister said, "and takes control of the bridges at Windsor and Sarnia, and barricades the Detroit Tunnel, we can keep them out of Canada."

Them? Aiken felt an itch at his temple; he sensed warmness approaching. He fingered his forehead in absent-minded fashion. Paris noted the movement and rose from her place, pulled into the chair beside him, and placed her hand over his. The prickling sensation left him.

"I heard they stole parachutes from the Army-Navy store," the Shift Attendant said. No one answered. "Holy shit," he said, jumping up. "Can you people imagine—10,000 pissed-off, sexed-up coloured men parachuting into Windsor with their pants dropped down around their ankles and their frillies whipped out before they even land?"

Their frillies?

No one spoke for several seconds. One woman suddenly rose and ran to her room, sobbing; another woman smiled, pulled a pocket atomizer from her pocket, sprayed perfume on her wrists, and dabbed it behind her ears.

"Do you have weapons to protect us?" the Minister said.

The Shift Attendant stood and hitched up his pants. "I do, goddamn it. Electric-shock therapy to the crotch. I will personally sizzle their little black nuts off. Don't you worry about a goddamn thing, pal. Sizzled testicles will stop any black man cold."

"Oh my God, you're joking," the Minister said. He left the room, and the Shift Attendant rose and dropped his cup into one of the dish trays before heading back to his station.

People started to move out of the dining room, leaving for their rooms or heading to the lounge. Aiken put his hands over Paris's hands. "Come home," he said. "Grab some time with your family."

"No. Come to my room after lights out," she said.

"It's against the rules."

Paris smiled, rose, and twisted her fingers at him by way of goodbye. After a few minutes the heat in his groin grew uncomfortable, and he rose and paced the halls to give some release.

When the kitchen staff pushed into the kitchen, removing dishes and clearing tables, the clatter forced the remaining patients into the lounge. Because of the riot, the TV remained switched off during the evening news hour.

"Itth becauth of the riot," Boris said.

"We understand the situation," the Fat Man said. "The coloureds are burning and looting Detroit at will. They terrorize the city while decent white people pray for the police or National Guard to jump in and lock those rioting thugs away. They should shoot the scum down in the streets and leave them in the gutters." No one responded to his comments.

Even without the newscast, anxiety on the ward prevailed above all other emotions. The patients gathered about the darkened TV during that hour, some standing and some sitting. Aiken leaned against the back wall as he usually did. Everyone looked to the blank screen. The Barfly, a stringy, middle-aged man who plucked at imaginary bugs about his head in short, controlled bursts, leaned against the wall beside Aiken. The ventilating system above Aiken suddenly banged, and Aiken jumped.

"Tricky stuff," the Barfly said to him. "Don't you think, Ricky?"

Who is Ricky?

Trudy, the social worker, joined them, pulling up a chair. She motioned for the patients to take their seats, smiling and pointing with fleshy arm extended and stocky fingers stabbing in the direction of the empty seats. People plopped down into their usual chairs, except for the Minister, who remained standing, confused. A transistor radio hung from Trudy's waist, with an earphone plugged into her left ear. Her lank dishwater-blonde hair hung down, mostly hiding the earplug. Occasionally whiffs of music or dialogue would blast from her ear, and at those moments, Trudy dialed down the volume, but the radio remained clicked on. When people were seated, she spoke in a low voice, leaning in toward the group. "Go easy on the crazy stuff today," she said. People nodded.

The Minister, still on his feet, said, "Miss Trudy, you're in my chair."

Trudy looked up to the Minister but did not respond. After a few minutes of her dead-eyeball stare, the Minster glanced away and moved back to stand against the wall beside Aiken. Music bounced out from her ear, and Trudy dialed down the volume knob. "Listen up, all you precious patients," she said. "We will not have our usual loving social worker's talk today. And there is no need to raise your voice, as I have a headache."

Behind her, the Barfly made the universal sign for tippling booze, raising a thumb with pinky finger extended. People nodded. Trudy snapped her head around and caught the gesture. She smiled at the Barfly and beckoned for him to move his chair closer to hers. He did so, sliding it closer with some trepidation. "Oh shit," the Barfly said. "It's not what it looks like."

"Yes, I know," Trudy said. She pulled up the Barfly's chart and scratched in it with a ballpoint pen. "No visitors for you this weekend."

"Shit."

Trudy rose and waved the patients away, but no one moved. She took Aiken by the arm, and he walked a few steps beside her. She removed the earplug and said, "You must meet with the Administrator before he authorizes more therapy."

"Yes," Aiken said.

"When you meet the Administrator," Trudy said, "try to lighten up the mood a tad. The Administrator loves a good witticism. It'll go better for you."

"Sure," Aiken said, "a good witticism."

Trudy smiled and patted his arm; then she chugged out of the room, music escaping from her ear.

The room suddenly got noisy; metallic sounds bounced down from the heating pipes, and patients rose up from their chairs, staring upward. The pipes clanged louder, and the Barfly stood on a chair and tried to undo bolts with his fingers to reach inside the duct work, with no success. "Oh, shit," he said. "I can't fix it." The Fat Man twisted toward Aiken. "The filtration system malfunctioning perhaps?" he said. "Filtration systems are funny like that. All sorts of things in life are filtered."

The Barfly stepped down from the chair and he sat back down. "Double shit."

"Yeah," the Minister said, "and the television set showed fuzzy lines yesterday." Absolute silence blanketed the room; all eyes turned, riveting mostly on Aiken.

The Fat Man swung his head around. "The CIA controls the *New York Times*," he said. "That much is obvious."

Honey laughed.

The Minister's face appeared to convey understanding, and his face contorted. "Oh God," he said. "They need the advertising revenue from the military suppliers."

The Fat Man scratched down below, wiggling his butt at the same time. "The editorial writers pretend to be left-wing liberals," he said, "just to prepare us for the next big lie."

Honey began to cry.

The Barfly slapped his head with one hand. "Oh God, Castro is gay!" he said, "That's it, Castro is a flaming queer."

"And this is connected to the fuzzy lines?" Aiken said.

"Thee eye ay," Boris whispered.

"The CIA controls the TV?" Aiken said.

Heads nodded. "I believe it," the Minister said.

"Part of the military-industrial gang," the Fat Man said. "Surely you knew that? That's all rather elementary."

Aiken examined the duct work carefully. Then he reached up and twisted a knob. The noises ceased.

* * *

By Sunday night, the riot blankets most of Detroit's east side. Monroe decides that the looters now outnumber the souls seeking racial justice by a long shot. He declines to loot on principle and sees no percentage in revolt. "Would just be pissing into the wind," he says to no one, "—pissing into the wind."

While he hovers over 12th Street, observing from the second floor of a brick building, the radio tells him that 800 state troopers and 1200 National Guardsmen are now working alongside the 4,400 Detroit police officers already on the streets. He watches the police in action on 12th Street; they arrest anyone who is on the streets. He hears that 1300 people are in custody; all but a handful are black. In front of Monroe, one mile of 12th Street blazes away, a raging torch; 20 straight blocks of Grand River flame in the night.

Rumours surface of targeted sniper fire against firefighters and police officers. The scar on Monroe's face tingles constantly. He leaves his post and visits a blind pig just to be around people who aren't out looting or shooting. He drinks sparingly, figuring that a man should stay sober during a riot, especially a riot spinning out of control.

* * *

Paris lingered alone in her room, dragging her butt to the room's only chair, then rising and yanking the chair about to afford a better view of the smoke spiralling over Detroit. She perched with her feet wedged up on the radiator, peering at the scene through her knees while munching on a carrot stick. Her knees slowly swayed back and forth. "Damn it to hell," she said, jerking her feet down. Aiken hadn't decided, she thought. He was still mulling things over and over the way he did, sorting through stuff, pushing things about in his mind, and only a family crisis would drive him to leave before he finished his damn mind-sort.

She left her room and scuffed along the granite-floored hallways, meeting no one, and slipped into the lounge without notice. Five people mustered about the TV set in a half circle, but no one raised a hand in greeting; no one winked or nodded; no one acknowledged her by eye contact or gesture. She pulled up a chair behind the other patients.

Images flickered on the boob tube, dancing across the screen; it was some sort of pirate movie, Paris thought, with a handsome white leading man. The hero plummeted down from the ship's rigging, swinging a cutlass back and forth in large swathes. He engaged in spirited fighting, killing many, many pirates. Now the pirate chief appeared. He was a somewhat swarthy fellow, leading his band of swarthy men with the occasional black man thrown in to increase the ominous nature of the group. As always, Paris understood, good and bad boiled down to colour, just the way the world actually worked. *Colour matters; colour damn well* always *matters*, she thought. "Go get 'em, swarthy men," she said. Heads turned.

From the age of four, she had understood the nature of her particular curse: she was a Negro girl, a coloured gal, living in a bleached and frozen world. She had had no mother to guide her, and her father, perhaps the largest person in the world, had engaged mostly in baseball or church things but seldom in young-black-daughter things.

From the age of five, Paris had understood her double curse: she was a black girl in a brown community. Just 50 miles from Detroit and the US border, they'd lived in the coloured part of Chatham, where young coloured girls decided on the pecking order in their own group—an order invariably based upon the lightest shade of brown. But her skin shade had showed up black, with no shade of brown—just black, deep black. In that year she'd also understood about hair texture and about how her nostrils pushed out, additional curses to a young coloured girl living in Chatham.

At the age of seven, colour had struck again in her life, but in a different way. That's when she'd learned of the existence of Aiken Day: Aiken Day of the brilliant blue eyes, of the extraordinary, brilliant blue, bluest eyes, who sold tomatoes to her father at his Division Road vegetable stand. Those blue eyes had almost struck her dead on the spot. Aiken had never looked her way nor glanced at her directly that day. He'd watched her daddy's shoulders, mostly. "Shoulders the size of a Buick," he'd said later to her, but he took no note of her that day, the skinny black girl with frizzy hair and wide nostrils, standing behind those Buick shoulders, peering out at those blistering blue eyes. There had been no jerking the price up while selling to a black man, but Aiken hadn't cut back, either. Those damn blue eyes had wrapped around and into her heart, stomping it senseless.

After that, she'd studied Aiken Day from afar and learned about him from quiet observation: lying still in bushes, sheltered behind trees, and watching him pitch stones at a board every single day, hoping to become the best baseball pitcher of all time—the new Smoky Joe Wood.

At first she'd simpered in front of her mirror, posing and imitating those little blonde, fancy-curled girls in school who simpered at Aiken Day incessantly, the ones who whined and mewed, "Could you help me do up my skates, please, please, Aiken?" Yet her simpering had fallen flat—she possessed no real flair for it. Simpering did not suit her. In fact, she'd failed miserably at simpering, even simpering alone in front of a mirror. Would Aiken Day choose someone just because that girl could out-simper all the other mewing misses in his life? She'd put away the mirror and mused about Aiken Day. A blue-eyed white devil like Aiken Day might fall in love with sass, perhaps learn to care for a sassy black girl—and she came loaded with sass, loads and loads of black sass.

She'd constructed love with Aiken Day by showing him that she didn't really need him, dishing out the sass to him, dumping it on him as though he didn't matter. That's really why she'd sassed him, to show him that *he* needed *her*, even though she wasn't a whit interested in him, him being a white boy and all, especially a poor white boy from Division Road who spent his spare time throwing rocks at a board, dreaming of playing for the Detroit Tigers.

But then Aiken had joined the Essex Scottish during the war, mostly because she'd sassed him into it, and on August 19, 1942, the Essex Scottish had landed at Dieppe at dawn, and no one had heard word one about Aiken Day for two years. It wasn't until the Red Cross wrote his sister, Libby, that Paris and everyone else had found out he was still alive—alive, only trapped inside a concentration camp. Toward the end of the war, the *New York Times* had begun writing about the death camps, about what had really gone on, including Stalag 8B. During those years, those long, long years, she'd had no one to sass but also no one to love.

After the war, even after they'd married, Aiken had carried stuff inside his head, stuff from the concentration camp, but after a while she started her sass up once more, only not quite as often. "Kiss my black ass," she might sass to him at home, husband and wife stuff; they would egg each other on. But she was careful what she asked for, unless it was what she really wanted, because the next morning she might wake up with her nightie bunched about her neck and her body sweat-soaked with the smell of Aiken Day. And the feeling of softness for him would sweep her once more, as she shared a bed with her blue-eyed lover and once again lay next to the blue-eyed pirate, Aiken Day. But some mornings he rose before her, pacing—those damn 12 paces this way and then 12 paces that—and if she said, "Kiss my black ass" on those days, she received a polite smile and a faraway look in return, and often the sweat beaded on his forehead by way of reply.

The TV screen flashed in front of Paris now, an advertisement for detergent, showing a happy middle-class white family, the sort of family that dwelled on Victoria Avenue. *I never truly embraced life on Victoria Avenue*, she thought. *Why not? We lived the good life. We managed friends, damn good friends. I was the first black professor at Assumption University, making damn good money. Aiken taught history at Windsor Collegiate to the brightest kids in the city. Our kids attended school with white kids and seemed well adjusted. We barbecued good cuts of beef and drank imported beer from green bottles. Aiken bought a black Lab dog for the kids. We lived the good life, the easy life—goddamn Victoria Avenue. Old Jewish women on the street, long-time residents, waved to me, like I belonged. Goddamn Victoria Avenue. Living there with a blue-eyed hero from the war and two black kids, a great job, green bottles of beer, steaks barbecuing, and a black Lab dog. Goddamn it, why wasn't Victoria Avenue enough?*

But she knew; deep down she knew. Even while passing over the steaks for Aiken to barbecue, even while popping open the imported green bottles of beer that had tasted so damn good, she'd known. She'd known that across the river, in Detroit, on Brush street and in other places, the door on a late-model car from the suburbs flipped open every few minutes and a black whore knelt down on rough, greasy asphalt to perform oral sex on a white man for a five-dollar bill, when milk for her kid cost fifty cents a bottle, and she still had to pay a pimp for protection. She'd known.

Black people were setting Detroit aflame for the shame of it all, she thought, for the damn shame of it all. And she couldn't discuss the attributes of different Cabernets, or thrill to grilling thick steaks on Victoria Avenue, without feeling very much like the simpering girls of years gone by who'd mewed, "Could you help me do up my skates, please, please, Aiken?"

So exactly what should she tell a man—a pirate man with the bluest of eyes, the man she shared a bed with, the man she shared a life with, the man she shared children with—the man who'd spent four years in a death camp dreaming of just this sort of life? How could she say to him that it just didn't matter to her anymore; that she needed something more in her life?

"Screw the white wine, and trash the porterhouse steaks, Mr. blue-eyed Aiken Day—I've got to pitch in and help. *You* aren't black. This is not your landing at Dieppe under enemy fire. This is not your concentration camp. You fought your war, and it almost killed you, and I see you fight that war again and again, every time you rise early and begin to pace, or begin to sweat or even hallucinate. So what do I do with the blue-eyed pirate who loves our children and deserves porterhouse steaks, and deserves those green bottles of beer, and deserves a bouncy wife who wants the Victoria Avenue good life?"

But suddenly she knew. She knew. She was keeping him safe for someone else, she thought, and giving him one last piece of sass, so he would never forget her, no matter who he might take up with in the future. And she'd even say a prayer that he did find that simpering girl to warm his bed and drink green beer with. She could honestly pray that he would find such a woman. And if that woman couldn't bring herself to love two black kids, maybe she could at least be nice to them. And maybe she'd even feed the goddamn black Lab dog once in a while.

*　　*　　*

On Sunday, Monroe listens to the constant sound of fire alarms. By early evening he figures that the Detroit Fire Department has completely lost control. Fires rage up and down 12th Street and beyond. Rioting residents hamper the firemen, looters interfere with them, boisterous crowds pound away at them, and occasional sniper fire targets them. Monroe decides to stay away from all booze for the time being to keep all of his senses on the alert. The air hangs acid-like over the 12th Street corridor, stinging his eyes. He purchases a small handgun from a stranger for a few dollars. Smoke blankets large portions of the city. Gunfire is sounding as they do the deal. "Kinda reminds me of Vietnam," he tells the stranger.

* * *

At 7 p.m. Paris left the lounge, aiming down the halls to Aiken's room, where she found him sitting alone, watching with the chair twisted about, just staring at the smoke rising over Detroit. She smiled at him, and after a minute, she knelt before him and took his hands in hers. "Come to my room later."

"They don't allow that," Aiken said.

"Aiken," Paris said, "crazy people can still have sex."

"Your roommate might squeal."

Paris smiled. "If you made her squeal, you'd be on top of the wrong woman."

Aiken's lips spread apart in a grin; his eyes flashed blue. "Come into my room tonight, sweetie, and take advantage of me," she said. "You know you love my black ass."

"I'm gonna follow the rules for a while," Aiken said. "That sex stuff is just not a priority right now."

"Liar," Paris said.

The blue eyes flashed again.

When the meds arrived, Aiken palmed the pills, swigging the water and making motions mimicking pill-swallowing. After lights out, he waited for about 30 minutes and then sneaked down the halls and into her room. The sheet stretched across her chest, with her bare arms resting outside the sheet at her sides, and he understood that she lay naked underneath those covers. Her eyes opened, and she smiled. The sleeping form of Honey rolled slightly in the next bed, and he heard a soft snore. Aiken whispered, "Will she wake?"

"She popped her pills," Paris said. "She's drugged for the night."

The fire between them erupted in furious sex, mind-popping sex, wrestling up the bed and down, on the bed and off. Afterwards he lay naked, exhausted, on top of her, blankets and sheets and bedclothes strewn about on the floor. His hands rubbed up and down her shoulders and back, down to her flanks; he felt sweaty thighs pressed against him and remembered life as her husband, especially the good parts: the special parts with quiet dinners, wine, and time alone with her, the bedroom a passion zone.

Honey rose up suddenly in her bed and said, "Oh, wow!"

Aiken turned to face Honey. She was sitting bolt upright, her hands on her cheeks, staring at him. He turned back to Paris.

"She promised me her juice if I let her watch," Paris said. "I had to do it."

"Unbelievable!" Honey said.

Aiken laughed. "Shit, Paris. Have you no shame?" He gathered his clothes together in his arms. He didn't bother to dress.

"Do you want my bacon, too?" Honey asked Paris. "I don't want to cheat you."

Paris put a hand on Aiken's arm, stopping him. "You can still come with me," she said. After a moment, Aiken shook his head. He started down the hall toward his room, bundling his clothes in front of him.

The Shift Attendant scratched a notation in the book as he passed by and waved him to a halt. "You went haywire," the Shift Attendant said. "And now you wander about the halls naked, in search of adventure?"

"Exactly—a haywire episode," Aiken said.

At the far end of the unit, unnoticed, the Black Janitor unlocked a unit door and Paris Day slipped through the door, fringed leather shoulder bag pressed under her arm. She stopped before leaving and hugged the Black Janitor briefly before disappearing down the hall.

"Really, I'm fine now," Aiken said.

"I will make a note of this in the daily log," the Shift Attendant said. "The Administrator will be notified, and he will discuss all this with you in person."

Aiken reached up and felt the dampness on his forehead. "Do we really need to record this stuff?"

"Sorry, but we keep a bare-ass ledger, part of the ongoing record of the nuthouse."

"Right," Aiken said. *Meet the Administrator and discuss the bare-ass ledger.*

*   *   *

The Administrator's office contained no couch; no fancy diplomas decorated the walls; no warm family photos plagued his desk. He yanked the window shades closed as Aiken entered the room. On the desk a small name plaque punched out the phrase *Semper Fi.*

The Administrator tugged at his vest. "Park your butt in a chair," he said. "Either one." The chairs before Aiken presented as ugly, bureaucratic plain, sturdy, but tank ugly. The Administrator's vest struggled across a bulging waist, buttons stitched tight, plugged in place to the very last buttonhole. A framed picture of a man wearing a business suit was plastered on one wall, slightly off-kilter. Aiken squinted at the picture, trying to identify the figure in the photo, eager to get some sense of the Administrator as a person. After a few minutes, the Administrator pointed to the photo and said, "McCarthy. The guy is McCarthy, for Chrissakes."

Remembering Trudy's advice, Aiken nodded and quickly said, "Doesn't look much like that Beatles kid, does he?" He smiled.

The Administrator stared at him for a minute without answering. His lips pursed, tightened until bluish white, and then he said, slowly and calmly, "Take a chair, Mr. Day—either one. You get to choose. You can handle this delicate chore."

Goddamn you, Trudy.

Aiken gestured to the plaque on the Administrator's desk. "*Semper Fi*?" he asked politely.

"Marine Corps," the Administrator said. "Battle of Chosin Reservoir, Korea, 1950. Minus 40 goddamn degrees, 17 days fighting balls-up against Commie chinks in weather that would freeze the balls off a brass monkey." The Administrator spit on the floor and scuffed his shoe back and forth across the wet spot. He stuck his thumbs into the sides of his vest, one thumb in each armpit, pressing at the material. "The 'Chosen Few' the press named us," he said. "We humped the wounded on our backs while fighting off slants. Do you hear me, Mr. Day? Fighting off goddamn slants, carrying wounded Marines on our backs, and minus goddamn 40 degrees."

"I hear you," Aiken said, flushing warm. *Goddamn you, Trudy.* Aiken selected one of the wooden chairs, then chose the other, jostled it about, and settled in, slapping his back and butt about, straining to get comfortable, and failing in the effort. The Administrator plopped into his leather executive chair, slumping down, so that the back of the chair rose several inches above his head, sending off a muted, threatening vibe. He flipped a file folder open and tossed pages back and forth before speaking. "Your wife was on the unit," he said. "She was on the eighth floor. She smuggled herself in, somehow, apparently impersonating a nutcase, and gave you a warm send-off—a naked body send-off, in fact."

"Really," Aiken said.

"She skipped out of the unit within the past hour," the Administrator said.

"My wife left the unit?"

"She bailed out on you," the Administrator said. "She ran out on you."

"Shit," Aiken said. "Shit."

"I am producing," the Administrator said, "the note she left pinned to her pillow." Aiken nodded. The Administrator shoved a piece of paper in front of Aiken and Aiken drew it toward him, reading the message in his wife's handwriting. The note read, *Beware the April Bitch.* Aiken stared at the note for a few seconds. "What does it mean, Mr. Day?" the Administrator said.

Avoiding female dogs with calendar names is probably too obvious. After a minute: *Better give the mangy cur-dog something to chew on.* Aiken fingered the note and shook his head. "That's one weird message. Maybe it's code of some sort."

After a minute, the Administrator pulled the note back toward him and tapped it with a finger. "Did she leave a message with you, or with anyone else in the unit?" he said.

"I'm in the psych ward," Aiken said. "I'm on the eighth floor. No one leaves messages with crazy people for other crazy people. People on the ward hear messages from God or receive communications from space creatures. The guy in 4D speaks with his dead mother every day."

"Yeah, the goddamn psych ward," the Administrator said. "Of all the government departments I run, the eighth floor of this hospital ranks as the nuttiest. We only assumed control of this ward because the FBI is interested in electro-shock experiments, and we try to keep up with those guys." The Administrator stuffed the note back into the folder. "The damn patients on this floor should be tossed into jail or thrown out on the street," he said. "Shape up or ship out. And the damn doctor in charge speaks in a foreign bloody language. He never even served in the military. He wouldn't know which end of a gun to stuff into his mouth."

The overhead pipes clanged.

"Did I mention that before your wife left," the Administrator said, "she hacked her foot through the TV set in the lounge? An unbelievable act of destruction. Forced me to authorize overtime payment to a coloured janitor."

Aiken shook his head. "No, you didn't mention that." *But I sort of assumed that he was coloured.*

"Does the broken TV thing mean anything to you?"

"Spoil the TV, spoil the message?"

"Exactly," the Administrator said. "Who benefits from spoiling TV shows that everyone loves?" He rifled through Aiken's file. "Your wife cast her lot with radicals, Mr. Day. She has become the enemy." The Administrator clenched his fist and jabbed it out toward Aiken, then slowly lowered his hand so that his fist rested on the desk a few inches away from Aiken. Scars on the Administrator's knuckles jumped out at him. The Administrator observed Aiken's reaction to the multiple scars. "These scars are from my time as an MP," said the Administrator.

MP? Probably not a Member of Parliament.

"I earned these scars in the military police, interviewing drunken sailors in a hundred different alleyways on a one-to-one basis."

The overhead pipes clanged. *Military police. Right. That hangs together.*

"Mr. Day," the Administrator said, "did your wife ever meet up with a person named Stokely Carmichael?"

"I know very little about her civil-rights stuff."

"You understand," the Administrator said, "that this Mr. Carmichael is the number-one radical, revolutionary person threatening the American way of life today? Did she meet with this person, to your knowledge, or have dealings with this Carmichael man?"

"No, definitely not," Aiken said. *Well, not today, for damn sure.*

The Administrator waited without speaking and then dragged a cigar from an inside pocket. He chewed off the end, fumbled in the desk drawer for a wooden match, and struck the match against his scarred knuckles. The match flamed. *Holy shit.*

The Administrator inhaled, sucking and puffing until the cigar end glowed. He blew smoke toward Aiken, who coughed in response. "Does your wife support our war in Vietnam?" the Administrator said.

Better lie. "She never said."

The Administrator flipped the folder open again, reviewed some notes, and closed the file. He peered up at the ceiling. "Some bullshit people argue that our departmental staff should take education courses . . . learn how to be better cops."

"Sure," Aiken said, "more education can't hurt."

"I never needed much education," the Administrator said. "The only diploma that ever worked for me was an 18-inch nightstick, or maybe a solid lead pipe with a few inches of black electrical tape wrapped around to give a better grip."

The overhead pipes clanged. *No repression here.*

The Administrator flourished his knuckle scars at Aiken again and rapped the desk a few more times. "You joined up," he said, "fought for your country during the war, and spent time in a prison camp, so you must believe in these things."

"Then it must go without saying."

The Administrator tapped his fingers, waiting, allowing time for Aiken to reconsider or expand on his answer. Aiken reviewed the options in his mind. "Well," Aiken said, "it's a crying shame about television and that sort of stuff."

The Administrator relaxed somewhat. "Completely ruined an $82 colour set," said the Administrator. "Absolutely killed it. Why does she hate the TV? The patients love it."

"A coloured set?" Aiken said. "Must be something in her background, only thing that strikes a chord."

"Give me something more, Mr. Day," the Administrator said. "Both the local authorities and the white-coaters give in to my wishes, and some of my wishes can make your life better or worse on this unit." Aiken shrugged. After a minute, the Administrator said, "Or you could be discharged from this unit, without getting the pills you need, thrown back on the streets with no hospital resources available to you whatever. With no goddamn meds."

Aiken coughed politely and tried to smile.

"Or," the Administrator said, "perhaps I toss some of your new buddies from the unit out on their ass—maybe Boris, the lispy fag, or maybe I chuck Honey, the ditsy blonde, out on her ass."

"All right," Aiken said. "I believe Paris hung around with a man named Stockly."

"You mean Stokely?"

"Right, Stokely—and she often spoke about two other fellows."

The Administrator removed a pen from his desk drawer and held it poised over a scratch pad. "Trot out those names for me," he said.

"I don't know their full names."

"Give me what you got."

"One guy named Andrew, maybe," Aiken said. "Andrew, I think. Maybe, yeah—but Junior in his name, also. I'm almost sure: Andrew Clayton Powell, Junior."

The Administrator scribbled a note. "That certainly rings a bell. And the other name?"

"Adam—or maybe Amos, I think," Aiken said. "Yes, Amos, for sure—Amos."

The Administrator scribbled in his folder once more, pulled himself upright, and gestured with his hand, a pushing motion, indicating that Aiken should leave, ending the interrogation. "Expect to see me again, Mr. Day," the Administrator said.

Aiken nodded, rose, and stepped out of the office. After the door to the office closed behind him, the silence in the hall seemed ominous. "And while you light matchsticks on your knuckles," Aiken said in the empty hall, "you can search about for Amos 'n' Andy."

*   *   *

It was 40 minutes later when the Black Janitor pulled Aiken aside and said, "Your father-in-law is stuck in Detroit and says you should call him." He shoved a piece of paper into Aiken's hand; it had a Detroit phone number scratched on it. The Black Janitor nodded toward Dr. Sam's office. "It's empty, but be quick."

Aiken plopped into Dr. Sam's chair and phoned Mayhem Chase. "Aiken," Mayhem said, "I'm in downtown Detroit, and they're killing people here."

"Yeah. The town's on fire too, in case you hadn't noticed."

"Honest people are breaking into stores for a TV set or better clothes. These people aren't rioting for civil rights. They're just looting. And the Detroit cops are arresting any black face they see—don't matter if they done something or not."

"Well, get the hell out of there."

"They burnt my church bus up," Mayhem said.

"Well, get the hell out of there."

"Meet me at Detroit Recorder's Court and bring all the money you can round up. We got to help some friends of mine." The phone went dead.

Aiken called Magistrate Frederick at home. "It's me, Aiken."

"Always glad to talk with a fellow Stalag 8B buddy."

"I need some help to travel to Detroit. Some muscle."

"I'll see what I can do."

Back in his room, Aiken found Honey sitting on his bed. "Paris, or Linda, is gone forever," she said. Tears rolled down her cheeks. Aiken pulled on trousers, yanked on his shirt, and grabbed his wallet.

"I could watch you dress and undress forever," Honey said. She giggled. "Especially the undressing."

"Stay here in the room for a few minutes after I leave," Aiken said. "Soak the blankets with buckets of tears, or laugh your ass off and piss your pants in hilarity. Do whatever strikes your fancy."

Aiken slipped out of the room. In the hall, the Shift Attendant glanced up from his newspaper, taking note of the twenty-dollar bill that poked out between Aiken's fingers.

"I might go out and walk the dog," Aiken said. The Shift Attendant glanced about, seeking confirmation that no one hung close, or not close enough to observe the transaction. He palmed the twenty and buzzed Aiken out of the unit.

* * *

Upon discovering that Aiken Day no longer resided on the psych ward, the Administrator rode the elevator to the eighth floor and personally discharged Honey and Boris. He rode the elevator down with them and pushed them out of the building, leaving them at the Ouellette Avenue entranceway wearing hospital gowns and cloth slippers. He passed over their clothes and personal belongings to them in white laundry bags. "Keep the bags," he said, "as a parting gift."

"I need my meds," Honey said.

The Administrator smiled and shook his head. "Go suck up to your commie friends for anything you need."

"Marxist-Leninist," Honey said.

"Piss off, little girl."

Honey began to cry. The Administrator shooed them away with his hands. Honey slipped her hand into Boris's hand, but they remained on the hospital steps. The Administrator spun about and marched back into the hospital.

"He'th a mean man," Boris said. "A mean, mean man."

Honey laughed.

*   *   *

Aiken crossed the border with his friend and brother-in-law, Winston Baker, and two other former inmates of Stalag 8B: Harley Pedrick, generally acknowledged as the toughest man in Stalag 8B, and William Frank, a smaller chap but still considered a hard-hitting man. Each of the three men stuffed a shotgun into the trunk of Aiken's Chevy. After skipping through customs, they pulled over and retrieved the weapons. They drove down empty, barren, rubble-strewn streets on the way to the courthouse, shotguns upright, resting on the floorboards, clearly visible. The only other cars about were police cars crammed with officers welding shotguns and carbines—officers who ignored any car with white occupants, even those with visible shotguns. Smoke rose in the distance, but Aiken avoided the riot zone and drove directly to the courthouse, where he parked and went to seek out his father-in-law.

Detroit Recorder's Court

The riot festered as it spread, and the police reacted with their own riot. They beat and arrested anyone who crossed into their line of sight, anyone who looked suspicious—mostly *black* suspicious people—black suspicious people by the hundreds, in fact. The arrested people funnelled into Detroit Recorder's Court for processing. The sitting judge heard an outline, often a very scanty, murky outline of the allegations, before setting bail. A parade of black men, sprinkled with the occasional black woman and dotted with the occasional white scruffy derelict, skulked through the courtroom, hour after hour. The court staff struggled to stay awake, cranky to a soul. After long hours of sitting, setting the terms of release, fixing bail for prisoner after prisoner with only two quick bathroom breaks, the judge's ass was burning; his hemorrhoids flamed in pain, irritating no matter how he parked his butt, and it made him edgy as hell and feisty to no end.

Aiken caught sight of the shoulders of Mayhem Chase first: shoulders that swamped every other dimension of the good preacher; they were broad, unending shoulders. But Aiken knew from experience that Mayhem's steady demeanour actually stuck longer with people; his persistent calmness, his ongoing absence of serious anger, his ability to wrench down his temper and display quiet composure—all these things shone quietly but stayed with people. Mayhem, wearing his dark preaching suit, waved at Aiken outside the building and dragged him inside, where they huddled at the back of the courtroom, a courtroom stuffed to bursting. The prisoner's box crammed 12 to 15 men inside, and when a case finished and the defendant was led away, the police pushed in yet another black prisoner.

Mayhem whispered to Aiken, "If they charge a man with sniping, the bail gets set at 200 grand, and if they charge him with looting, the bail is 25 grand. How much money did you bring?"

"Thirty-two dollars."

"Shit, we can't make bail for someone's shoe." After a minute, Mayhem said, "I'm hereby appointing you assistant pastor to the Chatham Baptist Church. I got five parishioners coming up for bail, and the judge probably don't want to hear from a big black guy, even one wearing a Sunday preaching suit." He slipped out of his suit jacket and helped slide it onto Aiken's shoulders. "These men got families at home, and they ain't done nothing wrong."

"What if he asks me questions about praying or about the Bible?"

Mayhem shrugged. "Just remember: they're all Christian family men from Chatham. We were just distributing food."

Mayhem pointed out to Aiken the five Chatham men in the box. When the first man came before the judge, Aiken pushed to the front of the courtroom and raised a hand.

"What?" the judge said.

"I'm the assistant pastor of Chatham Baptist Church," Aiken said. "This man is a parishioner, and I'd like to speak for him."

The judge nodded, so Aiken continued. "And there's four others from the church too."

"Have them step forward," the judge said. He shifted his butt and winced.

The five men shuffled about and lined up at the front of the prisoner's box. Aiken looked at the five closely. The clothing on each man carried rips and tears; each man showed visible cuts and abrasions.

Mayhem Chase leaned forward and said to Aiken, "They didn't look like that before being arrested."

The judge slapped his gavel down. "Who is that big coloured man who keeps talking at you?"

Aiken turned his head toward Mayhem. "This is the regular minister of the church, the Reverend Mayhem Chase," he said. Mayhem stood up and bobbed his head politely and moved to stand close to Aiken. He crossed his arms in front of him, bobbed his head again, and then placed his hands one on the other in front of him, in ministerial fashion.

The judge shifted in his seat, his face grimacing in pain, and Aiken took note of the scowl. *This guy is going to hang one of us.*

"So you're wearing the coat that matches his trousers," the judge said. "Do you two share underpants, as well?"

"Pardon?" Aiken said.

"These five men," Mayhem said, gesturing to the prisoners, "are all good Christian Chatham men."

"What in hell is a Chatham man? Come on, goddamn it! We got a few hundred people behind you, all in custody, all crammed into holding cells, all smelling someone else's sweat, all lining up just to take a piss."

"Chatham," Mayhem said slowly, "is a quiet Canadian city 40 miles from Windsor."

"So why are Canadians burning down Detroit?" the judge said. "Some kind of hockey party that blew out of hand?"

"It was about food, Your Honour," Mayhem said.

"So they were stealing food?"

Mayhem stood up straighter, exhaling slowly before replying. "Our church raises money and buys food and distributes that food in the Detroit ghetto."

"And you can prove this how?" the judge said.

The courtroom fell silent.

"Well?" the judge said.

"They're honest men, Your Honour," Aiken said.

"And I know this how?" the judge said. "Speed it up."

Silence dripped from every corner, wrapping about everyone in the room. *Shit. We are all going to jail. Think, for Christ's sake—ah!* "Look at their shoes," Aiken said.

"What?"

"Please, Your Honour," Aiken said. "Have a look at their shoes."

"You five step out of the box," the judge said. The two police officers closest to the box each placed a hand on his holstered revolver. One by one the men filed out. Each of them wore leather dress shoes; every shoe showed traces of a shine.

"Those are Sunday go-to-meeting shoes," Aiken said. "These men were on church affairs, and they dressed proper for it."

The judge looked down at the shoes. "So they are. I set bail at one dollar for each of the accused in question."

"We have $27 left," Aiken said to Mayhem. "Maybe Stokely needs bailing out?"

Outside of court Mayhem said, "Shit! Shoes! Anyone wearing sneakers would be in Jackson State Prison now, probably sitting on death row waiting for his last meal."

"Get your five buds together," Aiken said. "Follow us close. We'll drive to Port Huron and cross the border though Sarnia. And try not to piss off the border guards. Take your coat back, and try to look religious, goddamn it. We ain't home yet—and you owe me five bucks."

Tuesday, July 25, 1967

Victoria Avenue homes in their essence, at their very core, strove to achieve stateliness. While perhaps not so fine as the homes across the river in Grosse Pointe Woods or Grosse Pointe Farms, Victoria Avenue homes shone in comparison to most Canadian homes. The enclave of outsized houses possessed a certain cachet that few other areas of the city could match. The homes were appropriately aged to avoid the dreaded taint of fad, yet well enough maintained to avoid the dreaded rot of neglect. In short, these were homes that might properly house Canadian royalty—professional hockey players, whiskey barons, and the occasional lumber merchant.

At 3 a.m., Aiken popped awake in his own bed on Victoria Avenue from a deep but troubled sleep, a delayed wakeup response to the frantic pounding on his front door and the relentless ringing of the doorbell. *Paris?* He jumped down the stairs two at a time and flung the door open. Boris and Honey were huddled together on the porch.

"What do you want?" he said. Tears dribbled down Honey's face. Boris squeezed his laundry bag and cuddled it to his chest. "Shit," Aiken said. He motioned them inside and steered both up the stairs. At the top of the stairs, he pointed to a door for Boris. "Use my son's bedroom." Stepping a few feet further down the hall, he stabbed a finger toward a second door, for Honey. "You," he said, "use my daughter's room."

"Poor Paris; we mustn't disturb her," Honey said.

"Paris is out storming the Bastille," Aiken said.

Honey's eyes opened wide. "But your children?"

"With their grandfather in Chatham."

"Oh really," Honey said. "So, maybe there's an empty spot, a vacancy in the house—maybe an opening on precious Victoria Avenue?" She dipped her head down and smiled up at Aiken.

"Shit," Aiken said. He left the two of them huddled together in the upstairs hall, returned to his bedroom, and slammed the door behind him. "Goddamn you, Paris Chase," he said. "Goddamn you to hell."

At 5 a.m., Aiken, wide awake for the previous hour, pushed the covers aside and swung his legs out of the bed. He jerked on a pair of Levi's jeans, slipped into dark brown penny loafers, and stretched into his favourite Donegal tweed sweater. He stole quietly downstairs, but the phone rang out, and he grabbed it up on the second ring.

"I knew you'd be up and about," Paris said, "and wearing your Donegal tweed."

"What's up?" he said.

"I've got a new boyfriend," Paris said. "A man of action. A man who carries a gun."

"You move awfully fast."

"Stay in your Victoria Avenue cocoon," Paris said. "It suits you."

"Stay in the revolution," Aiken said. "Dress in military fatigues. Maybe do the Afro thing with your hair. All those things suit you and blur you up about the important things in life."

"You lost more than four years in Stalag 8B," Paris said. "Maybe you should move on. By the way, I left a present for you on the hall table." He twisted his head and saw the ring resting on the small table. *Her wedding band.*

Aiken was quiet for a minute. Then he said, "Go and save the world. I can raise my kids. Yes, I said 'my kids.' I can raise them without your help, since I always did it without your help. Go and nurture the revolution. Give it a hug for me. Sleep with it if you want. I hope it keeps you warm at night."

"As warm as Donegal tweed, you son of a bitch," she said. The phone went dead.

It's like mucking about the goddamn flower shop when she's pissed off at you. The brain says, "Send some dead weeds, together with a serious death threat," while the heart screams, "Throw some fancy roses at her, just because she's so damn pretty and smells of lilac"—and down below the goddamn sequoia stick bounces against the undershorts, not really caring about the process, just saying press on with the dogfight so we can jumpstart the make-up session. Paris, goddamn you!

His eyes focused on the gold ring sitting on the table, resting alone in the exact centre of the lace doily. It matched the one on his finger. He turned and climbed back up the stairs, crept into his daughter's room, and shook Honey's shoulder. She rolled over and smiled up at him. "Good morning, Aiken Day."

"Ever see a sunrise on Victoria Avenue?" Aiken said. *I'll crack open a bottle of champagne, and we'll see if you can replace my last gal.*

"Give me a few minutes to put on my makeup," Honey said.

"You need to put on makeup to watch a sunrise?"

"We're on Victoria Avenue, Aiken."

"Well, maybe another day," Aiken said. She rolled back over and closed her eyes, and a few seconds later she was spewing out light snoring sounds.

Aiken unfastened the front-door bolt, stuck his head out, and drew in the morning *Detroit Free Press*. Standing in the front hall, he flipped through the pages. The third page carried an out-of-focus picture of Paris. The caption underneath indicated that she was wanted for questioning by the authorities in connection with the riot. Her name was not disclosed. Aiken recognized the photo as one taken from her university identification card. He folded up the newspaper and set it aside.

The black Lab dog scratched at the back door, seeking relief, so Aiken trucked to the kitchen and opened the door, sidestepping the dog's mad rush outside. He lingered on the screened-in porch, taking in the morning and resting for a few minutes in one of the Muskoka chairs, his elbows on the wide wooden armrests.

Returning to the kitchen, Aiken plugged in the kettle and downed a shot of Bushnell's Black Bush Irish Whiskey to fight the morning chill. Using a whisk, he beat up half a pint of whipping cream until peaks appeared and then set the bowl in the freezer to chill. He went upstairs to rap on both bedroom doors a few times, returned to the kitchen, and pumped another shot of Bushnell's. A few minutes later, Honey pranced into the kitchen wearing a blue satin housecoat. She giggled, pressing her hands down on the material. "I discovered this in her closet . . . okay?"

"Sure, save burning it," he said.

"You are so funny, Aiken. I could listen to your jokes forever." *But only after you apply makeup.*

Downstairs he set the kettle on to boil. When it bubbled, he poured water over Columbian coffee using his Melitta filter. He positioned three cups in a row, poured a generous jigger of Bushnell's in each, dropped in a teaspoon of demerara sugar, and filled each cup with black coffee. To finish, he dolloped a scoop of whipped cream on top. Boris stumbled down the stairs to join them, and they all plonked down around the kitchen table without talking. Aiken dialed in the CBC news for the 7 a.m. roundup, and they sipped coffee while listening.

"Detroit still burns," the newscaster said. "Michigan State Police now patrol Detroit streets. People are cautioned to stay inside. In other news, the world wonders which team actually won in yesterday's trade between the Montreal Canadians and the Chicago Blackhawks . . ."

Aiken turned off the radio.

"Boy, it sounds serious," Honey said.

"Come on," Boris said. "He wath a rotten defentheman."

Outside, the black Lab barked once. "Puppy dog?" Honey said.

"Puppy dog has already pissed on everything in sight today," Aiken said.

"Don't need to meet puppy dog," she said.

Boris toasted with his cup of coffee. "This is better than cornflakes."

Aiken parked three glasses in a row on the table and sliced several Valencia oranges in half. He manually twisted each half against the glass juicer, grinding out the juice and separating the seeds. He dumped the liquid out until he'd filled each glass with juice. They sipped the juice in silence. Aiken finished his juice and began to beat up the buckwheat-based crepe batter, dropping in eggs, then milk, water, vanilla, and grated lemon rind. When the crepe pan had heated, he poured in the batter and flipped each crepe off in turn, stuffed them all with fresh blueberries, and folded each crepe in half to complete. He gestured, and they ate, chewing in silence. To finish off the meal, Aiken slid a bowl of mandarin oranges toward the centre of the table, and Boris and Honey began to peel down the skins and munch on the sweet fruit.

"Do you eat like this every day?" Boris asked.

"I had four years in a concentration camp to plan the menu."

Honey reached into the utility cupboard, dragged out a blue-and-white checked apron, and pasted it up in front of her. "Help me please, please, Aiken." He rose, looped the top strap about her neck, tucked the apron ties behind her back, turned her about, gently, and knotted the ties in a competent, almost pretty, bow behind her back. Her ass bounced suggestively. He put a hand on her bum and squeezed it, and she twisted about and smiled at him.

My goodness—a bum without makeup.

"Got to throw on my suit to meet with Madeline Claire, my vice-principal," Aiken said.

"We can clean this place up while you run off to your meeting," Honey said. "I absolutely love this home."

When Aiken passed through the front hall, he stopped to consider the ring on the table. A chill dropped down, tickling his spine and raising anxiety. He shrugged, twisted the ring off his finger, and placed it carefully on the table so that the two matching bands rested side by side, but not touching. *My brain tells me that it's over. Nothing to do with that bum—absolutely nothing to do with that bum.*

Windsor Collegiate, Windsor, Ontario

Windsor Collegiate embraced football and basketball with passion, tolerated track and field, and generally ignored soccer and baseball. But no student held the word *tennis* in any sort of sanctity, and the only tangible evidence of the sport resided in the unused, untended courts that reposed directly underneath the office of the vice-principal of Windsor Collegiate, Miss Madeline Claire.

Aiken entered Miss Claire's office and discovered her dressed primly, as always. Miss Claire possessed a slim figure; she was not exactly porcelain pretty; she was aging, but still handsome nonetheless. Her back was toward him and her hands folded in front of her. She stood ramrod straight, staring down at the tennis courts, in a somewhat regular pose for her. She remained still. The surface of her antique desk emitted a slight perfume, the fragrance of lemon oil. Nothing rested on the satin-finished surface except for one closed manila file folder with Aiken's name stencilled on it in bold block letters. She finally twisted about and faced him, crossed to her desk, and sat down rigidly but gracefully—far more gracefully than Aiken could manage on his best day. When she crooked a finger for him to take a seat, he chose the chair closest to the door. The chair squeaked under him when he lowered his weight into it.

Shit. "Excuse me," Aiken said.

Her eyes crackled in an aged but wrinkle-free face, with skin tight across the bones. Thin spectacles wrapped about green eyes that now bored into Aiken Day, threatening him and producing a queasy, fluttering unease that trickled down inside him right to his bowels. She removed a single piece of paper from his file and placed it on top of the folder, flattening it with her fingers and pressing down against it. The sheet appeared to be a newspaper clipping. "We must discuss the renewal of your teaching position," she said.

"I see," Aiken said. *Shit again.*

Miss Claire rose from her chair and stepped back to the windows, turning away from him. She clasped her hands in front of her and gazed once more on the empty tennis courts. "Such an elegant sport," she said.

Aiken said, "What?"

"Tennis is such an elegant sport, Mr. Day."

"Ah yes, tennis," Aiken said. "Almost too elegant, many say."

"Brought here by such elegant people," Miss Claire said.

"The Rockefellers?" Aiken said.

Miss Claire turned and faced Aiken for a second, ice pouring from her stare, and then turned back to the courts.

More elegant. "The Kennedys?" Aiken said, smiling.

Miss Claire twisted her head back to face him, the somewhat cross glare fleeting; she was too well bred to let him see her disdain in full measure. "The English, Mr. Day," Miss Claire said. "The English. We must honour the legacy of the English."

"What legacy?"

"My family," Miss Claire said, "descended from United Empire Loyalists."

"My dad had a vegetable stand on Division Road, near Cottam," Aiken said. "Onions and potatoes mostly, but some tomatoes."

"The English alone on the continent," Miss Claire said, "resisted Hitler from the beginning and persevered to the very end in the recent war. We owe everything to them. The Americans delayed and delayed, coming to the war late—very late—Mr. Day."

"But when they came," Aiken said, "they brought all those wonderful tanks and bombs."

Her face froze. Silence dripped about the room. The ceilings threatened to buckle downward and press the base human occupants into oblivion.

"Things without eloquence, Mr. Day," Miss Claire said. "Things with barely a whiff of subtlety or a taste of class. Europe, but really mostly England, brought culture and eloquence to this continent."

"Sure," Aiken said, striving for a conciliatory tone. "That stuff is never out of date; it's timeless, some people say."

"To elaborate, Mr. Day: the Americans produce machines, lots of machines, but greasy machines only, and this ability should not be confused with culture on any level. History teachers in this school are charged with spreading culture, as well as basic facts."

"Indeed, culture," Aiken said. *As a kid I spread manure, so I could spread culture. Yup. Absolutely.*

"Your salary from the school," Miss Claire said, "allows you to live on Victoria Avenue."

"Yes."

"Life must be pleasant on Victoria Avenue," Miss Claire said.

"Yes. Yes it is," Aiken said. "Big houses, tree-lined street. Everyone on the block landscapes. Not just grass cutting, but bushes."

"Fancy car?" Miss Claire said.

"A used Chevy," Aiken said. "Standard transmission but a real nice car—blue."

Miss Claire leaned forward, and her eyes flashed harder, locking his eyes into hers, and their eyes burned in lockstep for a few dreadful seconds and produced more unease in him. "I alone," she said, "decide whether or not your contract is to be renewed each year. And, quite frankly, I may choose not to renew your teaching certificate this year."

The heating system above them clanged.

"I could buy a second suit," Aiken said. "Maybe blue serge and a quiet tie, maybe red . . . one without a Hawaiian girl." Another period of silence engulfed the room. *Maybe repress the blue serge and buy tweed. Maybe buy a pipe, or maybe buy a woollen sweater vest in some bland colour. Christ, maybe tattoo the Union Jack on my ass. But I love living on Victoria Avenue. My life is under siege.*

"I am responsible for both the moral and academic tone of Windsor Collegiate," Miss Claire said.

"Yes, of course."

Miss Claire pulled the piece of paper that rested on top of his folder and turned it over. "This photo from the newspaper is of poor quality, but it seems to resemble your wife."

"My wife?"

"Your wife," Miss Claire said.

"My wife in the newspaper?"

"She appears to be a person wanted by the authorities," Miss Claire said.

"Hardly. My wife's on sabbatical this year, doing graduate work."

"Graduate work?" Miss Claire said.

"Yes, at Oxford."

"My goodness, Mr. Day," Miss Claire said. "At Oxford University, you say? In England?"

Not exactly a total lie—I'm sure Paris loves her Oxford dictionary, and maybe I'll start up a company to sell Oxford ice cream or Oxford hockey sticks.

Miss Claire nodded and opened his folder. "Now, on another topic," she said. "In the recent past, you failed to discharge your duties due to an alleged sickness."

"Well, you know," Aiken said, "I wasn't in the old psych ward to have the old noodle spruced up. It was more a temporary-assessment thing."

"About your so-called illness, Mr. Day. I wish to confirm that you will not speak of, nor bring up this topic for discussion, in any classroom or, indeed, anywhere on school property."

"Confirmed, Miss Claire," Aiken said.

"Insanity," Miss Claire said, "is not a fit topic for high-school children."

Insanity?

After a few seconds, Miss Claire said, "You will advise class 11A that you made a swimming pilgrimage to the Dardanelles, and that is why you were absent. This class is exceptional and will fully appreciate the classical Byronic reference."

"The Dardanelles?" Aiken said. "Did you mean the Vandellas, or maybe the Shirelles?"

"The Dardanelles," Miss Claire said. "The Dardanelles, Mr. Day."

"A classical reference," Aiken said, "is always appreciated by high-school students."

"I'm sure your time off," Miss Claire said, smiling at him, "during your recent vacation to the Hellespont . . ." A quick smile escaped from Miss Claire and then a sly wink.

The Hellespont? What happened to the Dardanelles?

"Political stability, Mr. Day," Miss Claire said, "and moral prudence remain core values expected from a teacher at this school. I fancy myself a *de facto* history professor as well, having read Gibbon, *The History of the Decline and Fall of the Roman Empire* in English but also in Latin."

"So, double the insight," Aiken said.

Miss Claire smiled. "Precisely," she said. "So we current history teachers must stick to the basic tools of teachers throughout the ages."

"Indeed," Aiken said. *Simplistic theories pounded into innocent souls.* "Maybe emphasize," Aiken said, "that Hitler killed the Jews and that Lincoln freed the slaves."

The heating system above them clanged.

"Yes, Mr. Day," Miss Claire said. "I believe that we understand each other."

"We do, Miss Claire," Aiken said.

As Aiken headed for the door, Miss Claire shook her head. "Indeed, Mr. Day . . . a coloured person doing graduate work at Oxford."

Don't bother to say it Miss Claire: Whatever is the goddamn world coming to?

*   *   *

Aiken returned home and immediately felt the absence of his family. He pounded a few ounces of Canadian Club over ice and clicked on the CBC news out of Ottawa. The announcer, brandishing his fake Upper Canada College accent, said, "Detroit police forces have been accused of being overzealous in the face of continued rioting. There are reports of many injured prisoners being taken to the hospital after being in police custody. There are unconfirmed reports that some police officers have removed their badges and have taped over the numbers of their patrol cars to avoid being identified." Aiken clicked the radio off.

Honey pranced into the room wearing black underwear, fancy lace stuff, and holding up a mauve skirt and a pale mauve blouse in front of her. "Aiken," she said, "Paris must have shoes to go with this outfit."

"I guess," he said. "Don't you need to get some meds or something, so you don't bounce up and down?"

"Nope, not since I landed on Victoria Avenue."

Take a memo, Aiken: insane people function well on Victoria Avenue. Honey is no longer on the emotional rollercoaster of the serious manic-depressive.

"What would it take to win you over, Aiken?" She lowered the outfit, displaying the fancy underwear.

How about unrelenting sex, hour after hour, day after day, week after week, with maybe a two-hour bathroom break at Christmas.

"Why are you smiling?"

"Nothing you would understand," he said.

"I wouldn't want a relationship," she said, "unless it was meaningful. A man has to be willing to go deep inside me."

How deep? She's naïve, but will she believe 12 inches?

"Aiken?"

"Paris has bags and bags of shoes. There are more shoes in boxes in the basement. Paris never repressed a shoe-purchase urge in her life."

"Oh." She dropped the outfit to the floor, ran to the basement door, and disappeared.

Boris entered the room wearing a sports coat, pale blue button-down shirt, and grey flannel trousers. "Can I borrow these?" he said. "I just met the most wonderful girl. She's been to a Kingston Trio concert, doesn't smoke or shoot needles into her, arm and goes to church every Sunday."

My goodness! Boris has lost his lisp. What the good life promises, Victoria Avenue delivers. "Borderline boring," he said out loud.

"Well," Boris said, "I'll just pump myself full of coffee before the date."

"Borrow away."

"And can I borrow your penny loafers?" Boris said. "Honey says they will set this outfit off. I want to make a good impression on the girl's parents." He put a hand on Aiken's chest, folding the material of Aiken's shirt into his fist. "I am so nervous about this date."

So nervous you're seeking wardrobe advice from two previous occupants of the psych ward? "Whatever you need," Aiken said. He hunted up the bottle of Canadian Club, grabbed some ice cubes, and pushed out to the back porch with the dog. The dog farted. *Back to my real life now.*

*   *   *

The phone rang, and Aiken picked up the receiver. "Let me explain current racial dynamics to you in basic terms," the Administrator said, "and then you advise your wife to turn herself in to me as the prudent course of action."

"Enlighten me," Aiken said.

"It is basic human nature, Mr. Day. Economic facts trump civil rights—always have, always will. People are happy when they do better than their neighbours. That's just how people measure these things."

"Really?" Aiken said. "Get to the point."

"It's the reality of status," the Administrator said. "In order for one person to gain status, someone has to lose status."

"Really?"

"A zero-sum game, It's the relative-happiness theory."

"Really?"

"Yup."

"But why shouldn't Mayhem Chase raise his status?" Aiken said. "He carried a man on his shoulders at the Battle of Dieppe and saved the man's life."

"Consider this," the Administrator said. "Suppose we give every black person from Chatham a home on Victoria Avenue in Windsor."

"I can't visualize you giving anyone anything." *Whoops! Maybe a lead-pipe beating in a dark alley.*

"Pretty soon," the Administrator said, "everyone thinks that living on Victoria Avenue is no big deal. They think there is nothing special about Victoria Avenue; anyone can live there. No one winds up any happier. Instead, everyone now hankers for a home on Riverside Drive."

"Is there a point to this bullshit?"

"When you give rights to a person, you take away rights from somebody else, relatively speaking."

"Well, these relatives are my relatives," Aiken said, "so back off."

"Look, buster," the Administrator said, "true progress in civil rights works like this. We rip off the asbestos siding from your father-in-law's home in Chatham and brick the house in—fancy damn brick, say white brick—and maybe stick in a stone fireplace, so now he can lord it over the other coloureds on the street."

"Anything else to add?" Aiken said.

"Just this," the Administrator said. "Advise your wife to appreciate her white husband. She snagged a great status symbol for a coloured gal, and she should race back to Victoria Avenue and screw your brains out, without any more crap. But first send her down to see me, so we can clear this misunderstanding up, and then you can resume your happy humping."

"Maybe I should stick in a pool," Aiken said. "Or maybe build a sauna for the little woman."

"Just pop for chicken or ribs once in a while," the Administrator said. "That'll do the job."

When Aiken hung up the phone, Honey said, "Who was that?"

"Just someone explaining race relations to me."

"And what did he say."

"Poor black people are the heroes of modern society," Aiken said. "They make white people feel rich by living in poor neighbourhoods, by avoiding prestigious universities, and by hogging all the minimum-wage jobs."

"I guess we should put up statues to them," Honey said.

The sweats struck Aiken then, and Honey crossed the room and wiped his brow with a tissue. *Right, chicken and ribs. Who needs a sauna?*

*   *   *

Around three o'clock the fevers in Aiken slowed, but by then Dr. Sam had confirmed the appointment, so Aiken decided to keep the meeting. On the way there, Aiken scanned down Ouellette Avenue, his eyes moving to the river and beyond. Dark smoke channels streamed above Detroit; occasional gunshots sounded, muffled. At 4 p.m., Aiken entered a small office in the Bartlett Building, an aging but still impressive building with granite trim, set in downtown Windsor, two blocks off the river.

Dr. Sam wore an unbuttoned plaid sport coat over a pale brown shirt. A bright blue cravat was wrapped around his neck. "Thank you for seeing me as an outpatient," Aiken said.

"My role at the hospital is monitored and my efforts at psychoanalysis limited by the Administrator in ways you can only imagine."

Dr. Sam waved him inside and Aiken slipped onto the leather couch. Dr. Sam parked his butt on a stool behind Aiken, out of his view. "In ways you can only imagine, Mr. Day."

"I see."

Dr. Sam flipped open a notebook and made ready to make notes. "Mr. Day, you repress things."

Aiken said, "Well, who wants to be known as that weird guy who farts in church?"

"More than that, Mr. Day," Dr. Sam said. "Your repressed feelings desperately try to climb to the surface but fail to do so, and in therapy we seek to reveal—to uncloak, if you will—these unconscious desires, the things that your mind tries to repress, those secrets of your soul."

"She has a boyfriend with a gun," Aiken said.

"Who does?" Dr. Sam said.

"What? Soul secrets?" Aiken said. *She's gone soul?*

The doctor lowered his voice and said, "Repressed thoughts concern sex."

She's having sex? "Sex with who?" Aiken said.

"With *whom*, Mr. Day."

"Sorry, 'sex with whom'?" Aiken said.

"This is progress, Mr. Day, tapping into your repressed thoughts."

The overhead pipes clanged.

"Things okay between you and your wife?" Dr. Sam said.

"Oh, yeah," Aiken said.

"Your wife would not be content to sit at home and knit doilies."

"Crochet doilies," Aiken said. "You knit sweaters."

"Does your wife do either?"

"She's a good sort. She's not always into changing diapers, but she knows right from wrong, and she's got her fair share of feistiness. It's in our generation's landscape, you know, stuck into our blood, propping up our backbone. We do what is right. I did it. She'll do it."

Dr. Sam closed up his notebook. Aiken remained seated.

"Something else on your mind, Mr. Day?"

"Racism, Dr. Sam. I worry for my kids about racism. Racism doesn't appear to take holidays or time off. What can I do about this stuff?"

"Mr. Day," the doctor said, "off the record, I own a German short-haired pointer. I purchased the dog as a pup. I never taught him to hunt, but he instinctively will go to the point position on occasion." Dr. Sam stood up.

"Wait!" Aiken said. "Your point about the point?"

"Oh! Bred into the rascal. Going on point is bred into the hound."

"So?"

"People have been bred to hate for generations—eons, maybe," Dr. Sam said. "Some fundamental urge. Something implicit in the human condition."

"But you could train the dog not to point," Aiken said.

"Nope. Shoot the bugger, put him down and bury him; otherwise he's just pretending not to point. He would be repressing the urge. Sooner or later, that pooch will instinctively point."

"My wife is black, Dr. Sam. Once I thought she was a full-of-life Victoria Avenue—type gal, but now I just don't know."

Dr. Sam did not reply.

"Your theory just can't be right," Aiken said. "There must be exceptions."

"You need therapy about this stuff."

"Yeah, write me in for next week."

"I had to put the pooch down," Dr. Sam said. "He started pissing on my wife's roses."

"I see," Aiken said. He thought this over. "Bred into the rascal?"

"Exactly."

* * *

Aiken rested in the living room, feet on the coffee table, alone with a Molson's Canadian beer, sipping in solitude. In the background, the Drifters harmonized on the radio. Honey tried on outfits upstairs. The closet door in the master bedroom squeaked open and closed every few minutes. At 8 p.m., Aiken's father-in-law phoned him.

"I'm getting phone calls from Detroit," Mayhem said. "The Michigan State Guard is now charging into the streets. Meeting in an armoury once a month does not make for a real soldier."

"What's happening?" Aiken said.

"Those Guard guys," Mayhem said, "are not even trained in riot control. Those fellas need to be tied down and restrained from what I'm hearing."

"Where's Paris?"

Silence. Aiken said, "My guess: Paris is in Detroit, mixing it up. She's in the middle of things?"

"Yeah, I'm thinking so."

"And the weekend soldiers are invading the city of Detroit and shooting the hell out of anything that moves."

"White weekend soldiers," Mayhem said. "Not many black faces in the National Guard. Things are gonna get worse in Detroit very soon."

Goddamn it, Paris, you left me, to go and save the world. Why can't my heart seem to let go of you?

Aiken hung up the phone and made his way down into the basement to hunt up another beer. After his fourth beer, or maybe his fifth, he stepped off the back porch and settled on the back steps for a few minutes, squatting, rocking back and forth on his heels. The evening silence of Victoria Avenue was broken by muffled gunshots sounding in the distance. "Paris is across the river, manning the ramparts right now," he said to the black Lab dog. "Maybe with a new boyfriend. Do we care?" He looked down at the dog, whose tail wagged in response. "I get your answer, bud. Thousands wouldn't, but I do. We should throw repression under the bus." Aiken turned to the side and pissed off the steps into the flower bed while the dog watched. "Between us guys, buddy." *No woman in residence, so no need to repress these basic human urges.* A few minutes later, Aiken phoned Mayhem back. "We better get to Detroit," he said. "Maybe do something to locate Paris and talk some sense into her."

"Your two kids need you safe," Mayhem said. "Anything happened to your butt, my grandchildren be lost—they'd be devastated. Detroit is just too dangerous for a few days, so we just keep the kids out of harm's way. We find Paris when things calm down. Help her out then—only thing that makes sense right now."

"Those National Guardsmen," Aiken said, "the ones you mentioned."

"What?"

"Something that doesn't get down to Chatham," Aiken said. "The gunfire from Detroit has increased."

"Shit."

"And I'm hearing the occasional explosion, to boot," Aiken said. "Detroit is getting more dangerous by the minute." He trembled suddenly as a chill passed through him, but just briefly; a few moments later he was fine. "And what do we tell my kids if something happens to Paris while you and I sit on our asses?"

"Shit. Guess I was feeling old for a minute," Mayhem said. "We'd better get to it. I'll stick the kids up with someone here in Chatham. Keep them safer."

"Get the kids settled and roust me out first thing in the morning," Aiken said. "And Mayhem . . ."

"What?"

"Maybe you should wear your preacher-of-God clothes to help us cross the border."

"Sure," Mayhem said. "My preacher-of-God clothes. Always a good dress choice for a riot. I wear my Sunday black suit when the real mean bastards are wearing Smith and Wesson or waving carbines about."

Wednesday July 26, 1967.

Nightmares flirted across Aiken's sleep. He rose before dawn, trucked his shaving kit to the kitchen, and clicked on the lamp near the window. He rested the small, blemished mirror against the window frame, lathered up, and placed a brand new Gillette blade into the razor before scraping his face. *The condemned man used a new blade, but his queasy stomach ruled out a last meal.* When he'd finished shaving, he shut down the lamp and noticed Detroit for the first time that day: the now seemingly perpetual riot glow bounced above the buildings, filling the sky and drifting in through the window; the muted sirens chased about the city across the way; and lastly, most ominous perhaps, the continuing thread of distant gunshots ricocheted through the air.

At 5 a.m. the phone rang. Aiken ignored it for a few minutes, but the ringing persisted, so eventually he answered it. "So a delusional Aiken Day heads to Detroit," the Administrator said, "to rescue his coloured wife with the help of the black preacher man."

"How did you hear that?" Aiken said.

"Part of the job," the Administrator said. "I am the good guy wearing the badge, waging the good fight, arresting hippies and civil-rights agitators."

"A wiretap on phone lines is against the law in some places."

"Just keeping democracy safe from the likes of your wife."

"What do you want?" Aiken said.

"My best guess . . ."

"What?"

"Your wife has disappeared into Detroit—the so-called black American city. Black, as in death. But I will locate the little woman, or her burnt, bullet-ridden corpse. And here is a news update for you, Mr. Day: 4700 paratroopers of the 82nd and 101st Airborne will take back the city in damn short order."

"Army paratroopers? The President authorized the Airborne?"

"Yup," the Administrator said. "My advice to you: take the day off and screw the hell out of that mental-case blonde job. I will wrap my hands around your wife's neck long before you cross the border. Your little piece of toasted meat is—how shall I put it? I know: toast. She is just plain toast."

"Let me know when you finally arrest Amos 'n' Andy?" Aiken said. "Be a perfect time to snap a group photo of the three musketeers."

The line slapped dead. Aiken hung up the receiver.

*   *   *

At 6 a.m., Aiken and Mayhem drove to the Ambassador Bridge in Mayhem's Dodge, threading through the light traffic on Wyandotte Street with ease. Mayhem wore his black Sunday preaching suit and a Catholic priest's collar as well. He tugged at the collar. "It's too damn tight," he said, "but I couldn't find no bigger one."

"You look priestly," Aiken said. "Black, for sure, but very, very priestly. So you might even know a Catholic person? Say, Mayhem. Do you know Bing Crosby?"

"I look black," Mayhem said. He turned about and held his arms out. "And I look priestly. But Bing never looked this good."

Not with his puny little shoulders, that's for damn sure.

At the Ambassador Bridge, rows and rows of sawhorses camped across the entranceway, blocking the path to Detroit. Police officers and customs staff shuffled about, some with pump-action shotguns, some with rifles, but some unarmed; most staff were just standing there to turn people away from crossing into Detroit, turning them back without discussion. After being turned away, Mayhem spun the Dodge around, drove the few blocks to Riverside Drive, and turned back toward the centre of Windsor, aiming toward the Detroit Tunnel. "More automobiles on Riverside Drive than I thought," Mayhem said.

"Pedestrian traffic, too," Aiken said. "Hard to figure all these people out walking at this hour."

People lugged lawn chairs and streamed out from side streets, jogged across Riverside Drive, and flowed into the park that skirted the river. Many shouldered picnic baskets or bags of fruit, and some carried bottles of wine or packs of beer. Even at this hour, spectators collected along the riverbank, milling in bunches. Some remained gathered from the night before, while others were just now settling into battered chairs for a view of Detroit; they collapsed onto air mattresses or simply lay in the grass. The sky brightened. The city of Detroit grew out of the darkness, and smoke plumes appeared across the skyline. Sirens could be heard, and gunshots sounded continually. "These people not just out walking," Mayhem said. "They're here to spectate."

"Maybe they couldn't get tickets to a movie show," Aiken said. "Or maybe this is the best show in Windsor right now. Or maybe just a good reason for a party."

"They come out to watch the low-life coloureds in Detroit," Mayhem said. "To see the coloureds shooting each other up and burning their town down."

"Well, that's sort of what's going on over there, right now," Aiken said.

"Sort of?" Mayhem said. "You mean them being the low-lifes and all?"

"Being all pissed about the situation don't help."

*   *   *

The Dodge slid up to the entranceway to the Detroit Tunnel, and a Windsor police officer waved them over. Mayhem rolled down his window. "Not letting people travel to Detroit right now," said the officer. He glanced at the sky and said, "What we got is just another American city up in flames."

Aiken, suddenly angry, leaned across Mayhem. "Detroit ain't just another American city in flames," he yelled. "Detroit belongs to us. It's a goddamn part of Canada. We own Vernor's Ginger Ale. We own Saunder's Chocolates and Joe Muer's and Hudson's and

Winkleman's . . . and Carl's Chop House, and Topinka's restaurant, and the goddamn Boblo Island Amusement Park."

The officer shrugged and leaned in through the window toward Aiken. "Buddy, we actually do own Boblo Island."

"Well, we ought to own the rest as well, so push us through," Aiken said. "Just pretend we're gonna jump the lines to ride the Ferris wheel at Bob-lo."

The officer straightened up. "Yeah, be my guest," he said. "Get your ass shot off." He waved them through, and the Dodge proceeded into the tunnel.

"Ignorant man," Mayhem said.

"What?"

"That would be asses—plural."

Aiken Day and Mayhem Chase wormed their way to Detroit through the tunnel. As they travelled underneath the Detroit River, nothing sounded but the whining of tires running on pavement; nothing glowed but the dim tunnel lights. As they came out of the tunnel on the US side, the sounds and sights of Detroit reasserted themselves and they noted the smoke streams immediately. The smoke broke larger and more ominously up close. At customs, Aiken and Mayhem flipped over their birth certificates to a tense border official. Mayhem's identification consisted of a folded, aged, official paper document; Aiken's was the newfangled plastic-coated kind. The official turfed back Aiken's plastic immediately, but pressed Mayhem's birth certificate into his hand, fingering the document. "Do you possess any weapons or firearms," the custom officer said to Mayhem.

"I'm just going over to give comfort," Mayhem said.

"I asked you about guns," the official said sharply.

"No—no weapons."

"Who owns this vehicle?" said the official.

"My car," Mayhem said.

The official pointed at Aiken, gesturing with his forefinger, "Buddy, if you want to piss away your life, you pile out and hoof it, but the darkie and his car drag their ass back to Canada. Detroit coloureds are rioting up the ass with non-stop shooting and burning; I see no sense importing foreign niggers to the situation."

Mayhem turned the car around to head back to Windsor, but Aiken motioned toward the sidewalk. Mayhem pulled the Dodge to the curb.

"I'm going into Detroit to have a peek at things," Aiken said, "and maybe hunt up Paris."

"Too dangerous," Mayhem said. "Wait for another day. Paris will survive. She's a survivor."

Aiken shook his head.

"Then switch clothes with me," Mayhem said. "Rioters might not shoot a Catholic priest." They exchanged clothes, stripping down to their underwear. Aiken pulled on the somewhat-baggy suit and the priest's collar, which fit perfectly. Aiken's shirt stretched tight across Mayhem's chest.

"Don't break those buttons," Aiken said. "I kinda like that shirt."

"Then why did you buy it in extra small?" Mayhem said. He pointed past the customs building. "Hike up to Brush Street. Park your butt at the corner of Jefferson, and stay on the corner. A friend of mine, Monroe, should show. He'll be hunting for me dressed as a priest. Monroe is ex-army, a decorated vet, so he might keep your sorry ass alive. My opinion only: stay away from the damn Administrator. I heard nasty things about that guy. If he shows his butt, stick with Monroe."

"Sure, common sense, avoid the Administrator," Aiken said. "But the priest's collar, Mayhem—how do I respond? What do I do when someone spouts religious stuff on me?"

"Ask yourself, 'What would Bing do?'" Mayhem said. "Sing that damn Christmas song to them. Or maybe, as a last resort, make them kneel down and pray with you."

"Shit. I don't know any prayers."

"So then, it would be a silent prayer."

Aiken nodded. "Right. A silent prayer. I could do that."

"Tell them something, anything," Mayhem said. "Frightened people or angry people need comfort. They're too scared or too angry to care what words are actually said, so a hand on the shoulder works—or something like that."

"Yeah," Aiken said, "a silent prayer would be my best shot." *Very goddamn silent.*

Mayhem put a hand on Aiken's shoulder, "Watch out for my kid," he said.

"Yeah, and look out for my kids."

Both men nodded. *Are we supposed to hug or something? What would Bing do?* After a few seconds, they shook hands.

The Dodge crawled back down into the tunnel. Aiken spun about and climbed up the Brush street incline. He then hung out at the corner of Jefferson, trying to strike a stance or posture to make him fit in, to blend better with a city in riot mode, but finding none. Eventually he just leaned against the lamp post. Few people roamed the streets. The ever-present smoke curls wafted above the city, and as before, sirens sounded in the distance. *Sirens and smoke in the direction of Grand River. Must be 12th Street burning up.*

After 20 minutes, a wiry black man approached. His face bristled with stubble and a three-inch scar sat permanently etched on his right cheek. He slid in beside Aiken. *He moves with grace and the poise of a lightweight boxer: wasting little effort, confident, bouncing, ready to slap a quick punch and bob.* The man's eyes flitted back and forth without pause. "Not many Catholic priests out and about today," the man said. "Maybe all down in Rome, praying."

"My father-in-law . . ." Aiken said. He spread his hands apart to about the size of Mayhem's shoulders. "My father-in-law, Mayhem Chase, loaned me this preacher outfit and collar. The uniform folk turned Mayhem back at the border."

"Mayhem Chase. Former ball player of note turned preacher," the man said.

"Are you Monroe?"

The man nodded, a quick, curt nod. "Mayhem too black to cross into Detroit right now?" he said.

"Somewhat."

"You'd be married to his daughter," Monroe said.

"Yup."

Monroe crooked a finger for Aiken to follow, and they shambled across Jefferson, away from the river, chugging up Brush Street but in no particular hurry. "Move slow, with purpose," Monroe said. "We don't want people to think we running away from something or running off with something," He pointed down the street and said, "Check out the armour."

The tank chugged ahead and rumbled down Jefferson. The barrel swung about, pointing down Woodward Avenue. The tank clanked ahead with dinosaur speed, the metal chains on the treads clattering a warning while the turret slowly wrenched back and forth. There were 10 or 15 National Guardsmen hovering about the tank, drifting behind it, weaving their carbines back and forth.

"Maybe the tank's to guard against shoplifting at Hudson's," Monroe said. "Stop all those girdle thieves. I hear Hudson's losing 100 bras a day to looters."

"Really," Aiken said. *He thinks people are stealing underwear?* "Any sign of my wife? Do you even know her?"

Monroe snorted. "What a piece of work Paris Day is. She clearly don't remember what happened to Joan of

Arc." He shook his head. "If she's about, we'll catch her trail eventually. Don't you sweat that, white bread."

*   *   *

They sloped down Brush Street, still moving away from the river. To the northwest, heavy black smoke drifted up, no longer plumes but almost a dark funnel, blotting out portions of the sky, fading at the edges into grey tones. *That smoke is whirling above Grand Avenue.*

After a few blocks, Monroe led him into Grand River Circle and then on to Grand River itself, where they encountered burned-out buildings for the first time. A few blocks later they trudged along an entire burned-out block, all buildings destroyed, now just rubble, with smoke streams winking off the ruins. A platoon of National Guardsmen stood spread out along the block, rifles at the ready, watching the smoke streams and making no effort to assist anything or anyone, making no attempt to challenge the scene. Black men and their women poked through the ruins, pushing sticks through the ashes, shoving aside muck and rubble, trying to locate keepsakes or things to help them on. *Maybe they're just trying to make sense of things.* The Guardsmen, all nervous and pacing, fidgeted. A few nodded to Aiken, but to a man they ignored Monroe, who kept his hands in his pockets and his head bucked down.

Monroe led Aiken down Grand River, and they paused at a row of brick townhouses still in flames with a group of people gathered about. A black man lowered a young girl from the second floor, dropped her onto the steps, and then jumped down beside her, while a lone guardsman, maybe 18 or 19 years of age, viewed them with detachment, not helping but not interfering. He leaned on his rifle, engrossed in the scene before him. Aiken and the Guardsman owned the only white faces about. Fires crackled from an adjoining building. Flames leaped from one unit to the next, the fire beginning to roar as it increased in scope. People swept out of the buildings, yelling out names, calling for the missing. Other people lugged pieces of furniture or armloads of clothes, but a few slowed to swing towels or blankets in a futile effort to stop the spread of fire. The guardsman watched and then began to pace, still not interfering or assisting.

"Homemade petrol bombs ended these buildings," Monroe said. "Do-it-yourself Molotov cocktails. No sense to this stuff. Most of these homes are owned by decent blacks—working people. Only a few of these are still owned by the Jews."

Aiken and Monroe soldiered on. The next block melded into small businesses, pawn brokers, corner grocery stores, and barbershops. A beauty salon caught Aiken's attention, where a hand-printed sign with the words *Hair Straitning* tilted in the broken window. The sign alone was untouched by fire, the building itself burned out and gutted. They travelled on, block after bleak block, deep into the heavy riot zone; most of the stores in front of them were now burned out, a few still on fire, some smouldering, and some of the ones not destroyed showcasing the word *Soul* in spray paint.

"A bloody riot zone," Aiken said.

"I'm not sure," Monroe said. "Are we talking revolution or riot? Or maybe a city whose time just expired? Maybe they should just let the whole city burn."

"They can't give up on Detroit," Aiken said. "It's Henry Ford and Joe Louis."

"And the sweet, sweet Gotham Hotel," Monroe said.

They kept shoving along through the desolation. Some of the businesses they passed stood intact, containing people who held weapons ready or men who blocked doorways with baseball bats. Some of these buildings were inhabited by blacks, but then they came to better-looking areas, with more brick structures. More and more of the buildings contained white men holding shotguns or rifles, with the occasional dog on guard. They started to see areas now with only a few buildings damaged and only the occasional one burned out.

"Now, the politicians speak about curtailing the violence," Monroe said, "and about saving lives, scooping up criminals, stopping fires. But make sure to catch the reports later, after the riot stuff is finished."

"Why?"

"After things is over," Monroe said, "governments count the dead, but only for history books."

"What?"

"The important stuff for governments and insurance companies," Monroe said, "is to take stock of the damage in great detail. Have to count every paper clip destroyed, ever apple stole, and each roll of toilet paper burnt up. They make a note of every lost dollar. But when it dies down, nobody's going to be pushing for any real change. It will be 8,000 paperclips versus 300 dead and 2900 buildings torched."

"So?" Aiken said.

"So, no one counts the suffering. They won't do that now. They won't do that in the days ahead."

"So goddamn great for me," Aiken said. "In the middle of a stinking riot, I get to hang out with the black Socrates."

* * *

At Myrtle Street, they paused to watch firemen fight a blaze on a three-storey building, pouring water onto a low, flat extension. Aiken pulled out a flask and they each sipped. "Ever get to the Gotham Hotel?" Monroe said.

"Heard of it," Aiken said.

"Truly the cultural heart of Paradise Valley," Monroe said. "Maybe even the heart of black America. Before the Gotham, there was no quality black hotel where my people could stay. And black people travelled from all over to stay at the Gotham. Langston Hughes stayed here and wrote some poems. Cab Calloway, Joe Louis, Pearl Bailey, and the Supremes all stayed, played, and strutted their stuff there. Nothing compared to it."

"Every famous black person except Satchel Paige," Aiken said.

"Oh, him too," Monroe said. "Everyone."

"Show me this place."

Monroe paused for a minute before answering. "It's underneath a freeway," he said. He spit on the ground. "With the rest of Paradise Valley."

They struck down a side street, turned, and pulled up dead at two fire trucks spewing water back and forth over burned-out and burning rows of townhouses. *We've slipped back into the coloured area. No whites about anywhere.* Black men and women, with a few kids, poked through rubble, searching for belongings, dodging streams of water spray, hunting small treasures—whatever they could save. The hoses pounded away, attempting to protect the remaining homes.

A middle-aged black woman approached Aiken. "Father," the woman said, "I lost the medal, my mother's school medal, from over 30 years ago."

"Things turn out better," Aiken said. He wrapped his arm around her shoulders, and she touched her hand to his. She appeared to be comforted by his touch and a few minutes later left to resume her search in the rubble.

"My goodness," Monroe said. "What a natural you are as a priest. Must be all the internal whiteness, bleeding through."

"Her medal must be under the freeway," Aiken said, "along with Paradise Valley."

A firefighter stepped back from his chores, propped up his mask, and slipped over to stand beside Aiken. Sweat rolled down the fireman's ruddy cheeks. He nodded a greeting to Aiken but ignored Monroe. "Hello, Padre," he said. "What a crying shame for Detroit."

"A lot of damage," Aiken said.

"Got over 600 calls yesterday," said the firefighter, "and today . . ." he shrugged, "who the hell knows? Snipers are targeting firemen now. They're taking potshots at us while we try to save their homes. What in hell is that about, Father?"

Aiken did not reply, and the man returned to the hose and resumed spraying.

Out of the fireman's earshot, Monroe said, "At the risk of stating the obvious, the people shooting those weapons don't own any property. And, sadly, few of them possess a Swiss bank account."

"Are you Greek?" Aiken said as they trucked along. "If not, all this philosophy stuff must wear on you."

As they continued down Grand River, approaching Warren Boulevard, the schizophrenic nature of the damage was again on display: some buildings were on fire but others completely unharmed. Gunshots sounded in the distance but also closer now, and louder. "Still folks in those homes," Monroe said. "Fires and gunshots nailing people inside from fear."

"Well, it's a damn riot."

"Folks not knowing how to act," Monroe said. "No one having a plan for this situation; wondering what's gone wrong—why God is so pissed off."

"Maybe the damn city actually is dying," Aiken said.

They travelled further down Grand River. Businesses in this area were faring somewhat better, but maybe only because inside every storefront stood a man or two with weapons, the men looking irritable, showing the strain of two days without sleep.

"Maybe class warfare at work," Monroe said.

"When a city burns down and people are shot dead," Aiken said, "people think of a riot."

"Maybe so."

"So, where do you hang your hat?" Aiken asked.

"Here and there," Monroe said. "Can't find a job in Car Town lately. I'll show you my best reference." He pulled up his shirt and displayed an ugly scar that cut across his entire chest.

"That's plug ugly."

"I fought in the big war," Monroe said. "North Africa, but I also fought in Korea. I'm 42 years old. I own two Purple Heart medals, which you can't borrow against or trade for food, and I can't get a real job to save my black ass."

"Yeah," Aiken said. *My wife has a black ass.*

"Bit of a rough patch, but I'll survive."

"Maybe you can fall back on the philosophy stuff."

A quick smile from Monroe. "Maybe so."

The two men strode along Linwood Avenue and paused in front of the Sacred Heart Seminary to rest. The statue of Jesus standing in front of the seminary had a coat of black paint smeared across its white face. "Shit," Monroe said. "Someone making a statement. People always making some sort of statement, when they ought to be holding down a job and paying taxes."

*   *   *

At 11 a.m., as they headed north on 12th Street, they approached a major crowd, maybe 200 to 300 black people, forcing a line of guardsmen to gradually retreat amid shouting and bottle-throwing. Monroe led Aiken back to Linwood Avenue. Linwood was quieter, with few fires and no crowds. A guardsman approached them, rifle in one hand, his other hand grasping the hand of a small black girl.

"Father," the guardsman said, "this girl got separated from her family."

"What?" Aiken said.

"Maybe you take her along to one of the churches," the guardsman said, "or maybe find a police station and help someone get her sorted out?"

"Sure, fella," Monroe said. Turning to Aiken, he said, "You'll assume care of her, won't you, Father?" Aiken nodded and reached down to grip the child's hand. The child played a nervous smile to Aiken. The guardsman wandered away. Aiken smiled. "Are you smiling?" Monroe said to Aiken.

"That statue back a ways," Aiken said, "just sort of screamed *sass*—a whole mountain of sass. Did you notice that?"

"Sass?" Monroe said. "Yeah, maybe it does do that."

Aiken pulled the child close. *And that sass reminds me of someone. The same riot that produces that sass produces a little girl lost from her family. It makes a man want to cry for the loneliness of it all.*

"What's the matter?" Monroe said. "You look a bit sick."

"Let's push on."

*　　*　　*

Aiken lifted the child up, and she snaked her legs about his waist. He trudged behind Monroe with his arms wrapping the child's back and her head pressed against his chest. Her only words were, "Find my mom." She repeated the request several times.

Aiken said, "We will, sweetheart," each time and hugged her, seeking to give her reassurance. At one point she put her fingers near his face but did not actually touch him.

As they poked their way through the riot zone, the child recognized sights and pointed down streets and across lanes. They tracked her directions, shifting away from the main burning district to an area of bleak buildings, a downtrodden area of Detroit where most streets and structures featured broken glass, brown, untended lawns, and bushes ragged and overgrown. Gaining comfort with Aiken, the child finally reared her head back and reached up, setting her hand to

Aiken's face every so often and running her fingers across his cheek.

Monroe said, "Maybe those clothes set on you better than you think."

"Just being neighbourly," Aiken said. "I got a soft spot for black kids."

They travelled until her finger steered them to a mid-sized building, a rundown affair with notable amounts of garbage strewn about the lawn. "No one lives there, sweetie," Aiken said.

"Nobody white," Monroe said.

"Nobody lives in a building like this. It's abandoned."

"People lock themselves in at night and hunker down, praying like hell to be alive in the morning," Monroe said. "During the day, kids play stickball up and down between these buildings, so don't call these buildings empty. They just empty of white folk."

The child directed a finger at the building once more, and Aiken nodded. "No trouble to check the place out," he said.

"Sure, I get you. We're already here—already down here among the garbage."

"Go to hell," Aiken said.

They edged toward the apartment building, stepping cautiously to avoid chunks of debris. One front double door tilted on a single hinge; the other one was permanently propped open by a concrete block. Monroe entered first, choosing his steps carefully, and Aiken followed behind, carrying the child. Around the first corner, past a vandalized lobby, they discovered an unconscious middle-aged black man spread out on the floor, dressed in scruffy clothes, with spittle about his lips. His eyes rolled suddenly, and he moaned. Monroe boosted the man up with little apparent effort and propped him against the wall, spreading garbage apart with his foot and steadying the fellow until he leaned upright. The old man remained comatose, but his breathing, in gasps before the adjustment, seemed to improve.

"Should we phone for an ambulance?" Aiken said.

"And waste a dime?" Monroe said. "We just hope the drugs wear off. Ambulance folks never work around here; too far down and too black." Mounds of garbage stretched down the halls in front of them, spilling onto the floor. Monroe flashed a hand to the rubbish. "City workers the same as ambulance drivers," he said. "They never make it down this far for garbage pickup. So junk, including people like this old man, just accumulate. That's what we got here—accumulating junk. Accumulating black junk." Monroe thumped his foot on the floor and then stomped it against the wall, banging the wall a few times for good measure.

"What?" Aiken said.

"A message to the rats: do not think that I am food. I hate rats."

"Any chance of the elevator working?"

Monroe laughed. "In this building?" he said. "Take a good look about the place. Use your eyes. Any elevator in this building crapped out about the time of Moses."

The child gestured in the direction of the stairwell, and Monroe nodded and led them up the ancient wooden stairs. No interior lights shone anywhere. The dark stairways and darker halls glowed only when they passed a landing; each landing sported a broken window that let in mottled sunlight for several feet.

"You understand," Monroe said, "that no electricity in a building makes for a somewhat lengthy and troublesome winter in the State of Michigan."

"People make choices," Aiken said, "or maybe choices are made."

"Yeah, white bread." Monroe said. "People make choices; people always making goddamn choices."

On the third landing, the ceiling wall stooped down, caved in, mostly, and Monroe booted pieces of plaster aside with his foot to allow easier passage. They paused at the fifth floor; it was the top one. The child pointed along the corridor to the middle door, the only door with faint light escaping under it. Monroe kept a hand on the wall and slid toward the door. He rapped on the door twice, waited a few seconds, and cautiously pushed it open. Inside the room a stunted candle flickered on a square clapped-out table in the centre of the room. The candle was packed down inside a hurricane lamp and pushed little light about. The better light inside the room spun in from the sun, filtered in through the small living-room window, which was filled in with a slab of cardboard pinched up and taped over in one corner.

The woman who stood plastered against the wall was wrapped in a simple cotton print shift, the plain garb showcasing a body with scant fat. She was all prickly angles. She eyed the window light briefly, stepped to the table, and blew at the candle, but when the flame refused to quit she pinched it out with gnarly fingers. She paused a few seconds. *She's rejigging her life, relieved beyond tears at seeing the child again.* The woman turned and spoke to the child. "Hello, honey," she said, "I'm sorry that I missed you."

The child wiggled for release, but Aiken held on. "Did you lose this one?" he said.

"Got separated from her, that's all," the woman said. "Lots of stuff going on in the city right now."

A flimsy metal folding chair leaned off to one side of the room, and a beaten-up couch floundered against a wall. Two wooden folding chairs were parked at the table. The woman pushed into one of the wooden chairs, with her arms outstretched on the tabletop. A small cut and dabs of blood marked her forehead. The girl squirmed in Aiken's arms, and he relented. She threw herself quickly across to the woman, and the woman scooped her up and embraced her. The child reached out and deftly ran her fingers along the bloodied spot on the woman. "I'm fine, sweet thing," the woman said and wrapped her hand about the child's fingers. She arranged the child in one of the wooden chairs and reached into a hand-knitted shopping bag, removed a single tangerine, and began to peel it. The child touched her fingers once more to the woman's cut. "I'm fine, just fine, sweet thing," said the woman. "Don't you fret. It's only a tiny scratch. We must take care of you, sweet thing." The woman broke the fruit into segments and the girl sucked on one portion at a time before swallowing.

"Out hunting up food," the woman said to Monroe. "We got separated." When the last tangerine slice disappeared, slurped down by the child, the woman hugged her and said, "Sweet thing, we best go out now and dig up some more food. Stuff is available right now, but you must stay close this time—only closer." The child hugged the woman.

"Kids are important," Aiken said. "The most important thing." The woman stared at him.

"I mean you need them to have good experiences," Aiken said.

"And groceries," the woman said. "They need food even more."

"Not much food around here right now, I guess," Aiken said.

"We make out."

"I could lend you some money," Aiken said.

"Go away," the woman said. "Thanks for helping my child, but go away. Go back to your own life." The woman pushed a small purse into her shopping bag. "Let's go hunt for some food, baby." She made to pick up the shopping bag. The child reached into the narrow drawer under the kitchen table and removed a paring knife from the drawer. She eyed Aiken briefly, pulled open the bag, and dropped the knife inside.

*   *   *

Monroe and Aiken watched the woman and child head down a street.

"Just a girl and her mom out hunting up food during the middle of a riot," Aiken said.

"Say, Mr. Aiken Day," Monroe said. "I bet I know where you hunt for food. You're a Joe Muer's kind of guy. It being such a high-class restaurant and right in the heart of downtown Detroit."

"I know the place," Aiken said. "Good food, good service. You know you've arrived when the kid takes your car keys, parks your buggy, and you slip into the side bar off the entranceway. If you tip the maître d' a few bucks, you get ahead in line. Then you chow down a great dinner, with unbelievable service, every stinking time."

Monroe smiled.

Aiken sucked in the surroundings, the fires in the distance, and the rubble surrounding them. "But I didn't eat there too often, though. It's kind of expensive."

"That kid parking your car was black," Monroe said, "and the people munching on salmon kind of pasty-faced, can we say? So we could call it, what? Say, maybe . . . a *white* dining experience?"

"The place was open for all, not just for whites."

"So you say," Monroe said.

"Yeah, so I say."

"Don't you fret, Aiken Day," Monroe said. "In Detroit, there'll always be a black kid to park your car."

"Go to hell."

"Hell? Nah," Monroe said. "Not hell, Aiken Day. Just Detroit puking up another quality job opportunity for a black kid."

* * *

Four sturdy granite pillars anchored the imposing red-brick church at the corner of Linwood and Hogarth. Monroe paused, lingering at the church steps, and Aiken drew up next to him. "Tired?" Aiken said, "Need a rest stop, old timer? Are the old military limbs played out?"

"Nice-looking church," Monroe said. "Do you sense religion hovering inside?"

"Let's move on."

"Do you sense," Monroe said, "a social gospel church? Do you sense the sort of black church that your father-in-law, Mayhem Chase, might preach in? Perhaps a church that teaches niggers about the social gospel? You know, the kind of message that black ministers pissed down on our backs for years."

"What are you on about?"

"You know the stuff they preach on about, Aiken Day. We can improve whitey and turn him about 180 goddamn degrees. Been hearing that bitch message for a hundred years."

Monroe stepped up, swung open the double doors of the church, and tugged Aiken inside. The silence of the church vestibule wrapped around them, paralyzing both men for a moment. Monroe set a hand on one of the doors to the church interior, but Aiken held back.

"Cut the crap," Aiken said. "I'm hunting for Paris, not a religious experience or a prayer meeting."

Monroe thrust open the door but Aiken still held back, so Monroe stepped back a pace, slipped in behind Aiken, and nudged him gently into the church proper. The gracious interior embraced Aiken, calming him somewhat. Stained-glass windows glistened, and sunlight sifted in, streaming across row after row of polished oak pews. At the front of the church, candles burned, making the light there flicker. Monroe gestured to a painting on the wall as both men turned to face the image. "Holy shit," Monroe said, slapping a hand to his cheek. "Would you get that—my God! What kind of church hangs an 18-foot high canvass of Diana Ross on the wall?"

Aiken brushed against a pew and folded down into it, staring at the painting. Monroe pushed in beside him, and Aiken slid over to accommodate him. "Probably means," Monroe said, "that the Supremes are gonna sing down here at Sunday prayer time. Be some great do-wop, do-wop hymns going down here, I'm thinking."

"You knew what church this was," Aiken said.

"Of course I knew."

"The Shrine of the Black Madonna."

"Good call, Aiken Day. And black people think you can't educate a white man."

"You think this has something to do with Paris?"

"Why a black Madonna, you wonder?" Monroe said. "Well, Aiken Day, some say, why a white one? Much like those white dollies that black girls keep, long after they outgrow their black ones. Why a white doll?"

"All immigrant kids face the same problem," Aiken said.

"Do they?"

Silence.

"Do they?" Monroe said again.

"I really don't know. Actually, I have no goddamn idea anymore."

"So you understand the theory in this particular house of God?" Monroe said.

"What do you mean?"

"Black people ain't gonna rise up by kneeling down in front of a white Christ."

*   *   *

Aiken sat on the front steps of the church and Monroe sat beside him. They passed a bottle back and forth. Aiken's flask of liquor was half empty when an unmarked police car pulled in front of the church. The Administrator stepped out of the car and leaned against the fender. When Aiken approached the car, the Administrator nodded to him in greeting.

"Your wife," the Administrator said, "is becoming quite the rabble-rousing firebrand."

Aiken turned back to Monroe. "You have no insight into my wife," Aiken said. "Paris will return to live with me and my kids on Victoria Avenue." Turning to the

Administrator, Aiken said, "And you definitely have no insight into Paris Day, and I doubt if you ever will."

"We will see, Mr. Day," the Administrator said, "who finds the little woman first."

"I didn't kill many men at Dieppe," Aiken said, "but it's like riding a bike—the skill returns when you need it."

"We shall see, Mr. Day," the Administrator said. "But I appreciate a good threat now and again." He dropped into the driver's seat of the vehicle and waved to Aiken. "*Now and again*, that is."

The car pulled away, leaving Aiken and Monroe alone in front of the red-brick church.

"About your kids," Monroe said. "From what I hear, looking like her and not like you so much would make them more her kids than yours."

"They could have been hers," Aiken said. "Maybe they should have been. But Paris was away so much, they just took to me more than her. And I get on with black kids, with or without this collar." He jerked the collar off. The Administrator's car returned at that moment and pulled up in front of the church. The Administrator beckoned to Aiken.

"Don't trust that honky," Monroe said.

The Administrator stepped out of the car and flapped open the sides of his suit coat, first one side and then the other, in exaggerated fashion, to show he was unarmed. "Take a little trip with me, Mr. Day," he said. "No weapons and no tricks. I can provide you with some insight into a gen-u-wine race riot." Aiken stayed still. "Maybe give you some insight into that black woman of yours, as well."

"It's maybe about Paris," Aiken said to Monroe, "even if he doesn't have her."

Monroe placed himself to block the Administrator's view, but facing Aiken. He pulled up his shirt. A small pistol nibbled up, sitting snugly above his belt. "Help yourself, Aiken Day. You can return it to the good Reverend Chase."

Aiken slipped the weapon into his own belt and pulled his shirt over it. Monroe stepped aside. Aiken waved to the Administrator. "Let's go, Mr. Bullshit."

* * *

Inside the Administrator's squad car, Aiken wired himself to the passenger's seat, pressing his feet against the floorboards, pushing hard, feeling pain, but finally relaxing somewhat. The Administrator rammed the car along at a steady pace, threading the traffic with ease down Detroit streets toward the heavy riot area; he whistled softly as he drove.

After a mile or so, the Administrator said, "The Airborne will stuff these niggers back into their place, mark my words."

"Just like fighting *slants* in Korea," Aiken said.

The Administrator turned and smiled at him. "Precisely, Mr. Day. Not all the slants live in Korea. Aptly put. Damn, but I feel alive. Nothing beats killing gooks just to pass the time of day." He slammed the accelerator to the floor, and the car jerked forward.

"Don't forget lugging wounded buddies on your back," Aiken said.

"Sure, what the hell," the Administrator said. "And saving the lives of guys dumb enough to get shot." The car surged, sailing along burned-out streets, rolling by anonymous black people who slunk along the city sidewalks with shuffling gait, slipping along in silence, trying to slide under police radar. Most of them were men; there were no young children, not anywhere, and only a few women tramped the roads. Random squad cars patrolled the roads with nervous white police officers inside. Their vehicles slowed to check out the Administrator's vehicle and spun away when the officers viewed the white men. The Administrator whistled away. Signs of a war zone jumped out on every block, desolation evident everywhere. Damaged cars with slashed tires streamed smoke, cratered buildings smouldered, and garbage and debris jammed the streets. Many a street corner featured its own cadre of guardsman, all brandishing carbines. Occasionally a tank with vigilant, but mostly nervous, guardsmen astride rumbled slowly down a neighbourhood street, with a swivelling turret threatening to bring even more violence to the streets. The Administrator whistled away.

After travelling down Woodward for several minutes, the Administrator heaved the car to the curb across the street from a mid-sized motel. He motioned for Aiken to remain in the car and crossed the street to huddle with two uniformed police officers standing next to a squad car. The Administrator crooked a finger, beckoning to Aiken, who quickly shoved out of the car, crossed the street, and drew up beside the cop car. A police officer with sergeant's stripes on his sleeve pointedly ignored Aiken and passed over a manila folder to the Administrator. The Administrator poked about the inside of the folder, shuffling some photographs about. He pulled the folder into his chest.

"The FBI," he said, "with my energetic assistance, is investigating—conducting an ongoing criminal investigation inside this building. They're concerned about several possible breaches of the law. Say, for instance, looting."

"Looting?" Aiken said.

"Yes, looting." The Administrator touched a finger to his heart. "I could find evidence of no other crime." He wiped a non-existent tear from his face and pushed a photograph of an obviously dead young, black man toward Aiken. "Take a good look, Mr. Day. Observe the results of insurrection." When Aiken did not react to the photo, the Administrator shoved a second picture in front of that one, and when the Administrator received still no response, he brandished a third snapshot: all were photos of dead young black men.

"These men were looters, Mr. Day," the Administrator said. "Ever see any of these three criminals at your residence?" Aiken shook his head. "To be more specific, Mr. Day," the Administrator said, "have you ever seen any of these criminals in the company of your wife?"

"Paris never meets with dead kids," Aiken said. "Well, hardly ever. She finds it difficult to get a dialogue going. Probably a failing on her part. Maybe it's even genetic."

The Administrator closed the folder on the photos. "Such a fine line between 'kids,' and 'looters to be shot on sight,' don't you find?"

"Something only a slant-hunter would pick up on," Aiken said.

"I am questioning a guardsman," the Administrator said, "about these deaths." He jiggled his head to indicate a figure seated in the rear of the police car.

"You suspect this man of murdering these kids?" Aiken said.

"*Murder* is such a harsh term," the Administrator said. "Care to greet the local hero?"

"Sure, why not."

The Administrator gestured for Aiken to enter the car, and Aiken slid into the front passenger seat while the Administrator circled the car and climbed into the driver's side. Aiken turned in his seat to face the man, who was young and white, with tussled brown hair. *Rather nondescript in every respect. An ordinary chap. Maybe 20 or 25 years old.* The Administrator turned about as well and smiled, chopping his head up and down for Aiken to proceed. "Did you kill those boys?" Aiken said.

"You sound pissed off," the man said. "I mean, over a damn weekend soldier job." The Administrator smiled at Aiken and whistled softly.

"I didn't do anything wrong," the guardsman said. He twisted his head and stared out the side window of the car. "I need to get home. I got things to do today. We might barbecue if the weather holds."

Outside of the car, the Administrator said, "This is a militiaman, Mr. Day. A hardworking fellow who sweats out life. He holds down a job and a works as a guardsman in his spare time. He supports a family. He has a mortgage payment. In short, he is not some hippie turd strung out on drugs and puking out his guts at a rock 'n' roll concert."

"So which way were those boys facing when they died?" Aiken said.

"Immaterial."

"Thank you, Mr. Bullshit," Aiken said.

A muscle in the Administrator's face twitched. "You just met with the hero," he said. "But off the record, the families will bury those hoodlums face up, so they don't have to stare at the holes in their backs."

An execution.

"There it is, Mr. Day. Detroit riot life in a nutshell. So toss that message along to the coloured missus: he 'didn't do anything wrong.' You heard him say so—so nothing out of the ordinary happening here."

"Why even pretend to investigate these killings?"

"Your goddamn wife keeps talking to these TV news people," the Administrator said. "Stirring up shit."

"So your officers standing behind us here, they all forgot to put their badges on today?"

"It's a riot," the Administrator said. "Men of action are held to a different standard. And it doesn't matter, Mr. Day. It just doesn't matter. So tell the little woman to turn herself in to me. What happened to these looters can happen to anyone."

"I'll pass that message along," Aiken said.

The Administrator tossed the manila folder into the front seat of the car. "You should be able to hike back to the tunnel in an hour or so," the Administrator said. "Better get hoofing. As a law enforcement officer, I can't go around spending government money transporting civilians about."

*　　*　　*

The two men spoke in Aiken's kitchen. Mayhem Chase nursed his beer. Aiken drew down on his fourth. "It's goddamn blasphemy," Mayhem said. He reflected on that comment and knelt down on the linoleum floor, arthritic knees tweaking, protesting in pain. "Lord, please forgive the blasphemy," he said.

Aiken smiled. "You can call me Aiken when we're alone like this. No need to be so formal."

"My daughter has to understand that a black Madonna is not part of Detroit's culture," Mayhem said. "And it's not part of my religion. Goddamn it to hell."

"Maybe you should just stay on your knees until this conversation is finished and all the blasphemy stuff put to bed."

"I miss Paradise Valley," Mayhem said. "I miss each of the 34 crowded, busy blocks. It was the heart of black America. It out-sparkled anything in Harlem or Chicago or on the west coast. These 34 blocks were stuffed with nightclubs, schools, and churches, but also good homes and proper businesses, and more ball parks. Life oozed in those blocks. It just oozed out and carried on living. Black living."

"A lot of nightclubs there," Aiken said, "as I recall."

"Yeah. And in my whoring days I hit them all: the Forest Club, Brown's Bar, the Surf Club, the Paradise Theatre, Club 666, and others. Lots of others. There were so many damn places to get in trouble as a young buck."

"They say those days were lively."

"Reverend Hill found me in Paradise Valley," Mayhem said, "a lot of years ago. He drew me in. He breathed the social gospel into me."

"My pa never held with church-going. Thought that church time took away from drinking time."

It was Mayhem's turn to smile. "That was him, all right." He pushed his beer aside. "He taught me that people can be fixed. White people too."

"Reverend Hill?"

A nod. "Before him I spent my days whoring. Doing nothing but whoring. Doing nothing good."

"And Hill got you a library card," Aiken said, "then taught you to read and write, and soon you could do numbers."

Another smile from Mayhem.

"And now you're a preacher," Aiken said, "praying on my kitchen floor. Just look at you now."

"Reverend Hill took me in and pointed me," Mayhem said.

"The man probably needed therapy or pills."

"There's more to this Detroit problem than is talked about," Mayhem said. "It's about what they took from us."

"Must have been a strapping fellow to take something from you."

"Before blacks settled here," Mayhem said, "there were others lived in Paradise Valley. First the French and Germans, then the Irish, Greeks, Jews, and Poles, in turn. And each of these groups moved out to better, fancier homes, and it was expected."

"The American way."

"But once Paradise Valley turned black," Mayhem said, "it stayed black, because we had nowhere else to crawl to. We were not allowed into the suburbs."

"Is this conversation going anywhere in particular?"

"So we stayed," Mayhem said, "and we made it into a sparkling Negro place, a place to live, to pray, to work."

"Don't forget the whoring."

"No, I don't do it no more," Mayhem said. "But I don't forget."

Aiken opened another beer for himself. Mayhem shook his head.

"White city administrations put paid to Paradise Valley," Mayhem said. "Urban renewal."

"Good old goddamn urban renewal," Aiken said. "Don't you love the lie in those words?"

"Yeah. I do love that lie. They razed block after block of Paradise Valley, knocked down churches and homes. Aiken, they paved over Paradise Valley for the damn interstate. They threw out Paradise Valley for freeways to dump white people into the suburbs a few minutes faster, to sooner spark up their barbecues."

"Nothing to be done now," Aiken said.

"This Easter, Reverend Cleage unveiled his black Madonna for the first time."

"It's damn pretty up there on that wall, Mayhem. Don't know about the religious stuff, but it is damn pretty."

"A black Madonna chills me deep," Mayhem said. "Jesus was not black, nor white, nor Polish, nor green, nor was he five foot ten inches tall."

"Don't go all preachy-preachy."

"Paris . . . daughter," Mayhem said. "What in hell you messing about with?"

"Paris will survive," Aiken said.

"This is my culture, in my church, writ basic," Mayhem said. "Christ is the only message. Salvation waits for us. Do not paint God in our colours. Human colours are limiting—far too limiting."

"Paradise Valley is dead and buried," Aiken said. "No going back. But it's never too late for sermonizing."

"The music and the dance are gone," Mayhem said. "The good life and proper religion, religion with bone-stomping music—you're probably right. Maybe they're all gone. But do you see what they left us with?"

"You're gonna tell me, I suppose." *And I ain't big enough to stop you, in any event.*

"In place of the culture of Paradise Valley, they dropped TV sets by parachute. Little white parachutes, with "I Love Lucy" blasting out on every TV set, and the only black people shown are clowns, like Amos 'n' Andy."

"That might change some day," Aiken said.

"No man ever learned to hit a ball, play trumpet, love a woman, appreciate jazz, find God, or be a proper black man by watching "I Love Lucy." Joe Louis didn't grow up watching "I Love Lucy" for damn sure." Mayhem slammed the beer bottle down on the floor and it bounced away. He jumped two quick steps, picked it up, and flung it once more to the floor. This time it broke and splintered. "Goddamn it," he said.

"I'll have the black maid attend to it," Aiken said. "Oh wait—she left me for a guy with a gun."

Mayhem twisted about, bending creaky knees to the linoleum floor once again. "It's me again, Lord," he said. "Please forgive another blasphemy."

"Don't call me Lord when we are alone," Aiken said.

Thursday, July 27, 1967

At 5 a.m., nightmare debris from Stalag 8B dashed Aiken awake. He dragged off the sweat-soaked sheets, stumbled about, and shifted into his fever walk, pacing the room 12 steps each way. A few minutes later the phone rang, and he fielded the call on the upstairs extension. "What?" he said.

"How to phrase this," the Administrator said, "without gloating excessively."

"Give it your best shot, asshole."

"I possess your wife," the Administrator said, "draped in chains, as they say."

"Let her go."

"When she exits the unit, her spirit and much of her brain will remain behind. She may even drool a bit."

"Let her go."

"Her future employment prospects will be limited to cleaning hotel rooms and taking out the trash, but she will be one docile and subservient nigger wife. And you will come to thank me."

"Release her unharmed," Aiken said, "and I may not kill you. And if I do kill you dead, I may not piss on your corpse." The line clicked off, and Aiken yelled into the dead phone, "But who gives a rat's ass—not a goddamn rat's ass about a missing wife with a new boyfriend!"

Downstairs, Aiken spiffed up the kitchen, cramming away cereal boxes and wiping down the countertop several times. He wrestled the kitchen garbage container outside and dragged it to the trash can, where he emptied it, pressing the bags and bottles down until the lid could grab. He flung the kitchen container into the backyard and left it there in the grass. The Detroit sky glimmered faintly, showing low clouds with muted colours. Gunshots from across the river still sounded at random. The flowers beside the back steps lay flat and lifeless. "Take a memo," he said. "Proper gentlemen on Victoria Avenue refrain from pissing on flowers for fear of repressing them." Back in the kitchen, he located the two gold rings he'd stuck into the back of a cupboard drawer, rounded up a tin of some sort of polish, and began to polish the rings, rubbing them relentlessly.

"What's a boyfriend or two?" he said. "And why am I rubbing these rings?" *It's because, deep down, I don't believe the new-boyfriend line of crap. Paris was maybe just telling me to move on, maybe find someone else to share a life with. Maybe she was pulling a Sydney Carton "a far, far better thing I do" guff. But is it over between us?*

He phoned Mayhem. "The Administrator has Paris and is fixing to do her some serious harm."

"Nope," Mayhem said. "Just got a call from the janitor, and she's been transferred out. The Administrator will have to pull wings off flies to keep himself amused."

"I didn't care in any event," said Aiken. "Just called out of respect for you."

"Spit out what's on your mind," Mayhem said.

"Paris disappeared from my life of her own free will. She has moved on."

There was silence and then, "This is not you speaking," Mayhem said. "Not the Aiken Day I know."

"It's the new me speaking," Aiken said. "Paris chose her road. Victoria Avenue is hardly a ghetto or a concentration camp, and hear this, Reverend Mayhem Chase. I'm like a pig in shit living on Victoria Avenue without her. I'm living like a pig in shit. I was meant for Victoria Avenue." He slammed the receiver down. *Goddamn you, Paris.*

*   *   *

Aiken's phone rang. "The schedule obligates you to supervise cadet uniforms today," Miss Claire said, "and you appear somewhat tardy in your duties."

"Yes, I was just leaving for the school," Aiken said. *Today? Shit.*

"Please see me, as well."

"Absolutely." *Shit again.*

Windsor Collegiate, built during the reign of Queen Victoria, was a solid, imposing red-brick structure built with the best of Victorian intentions but now somewhat past its prime. Down in the bowels of the basement, past the equipment rooms, past the compact rifle range and all the lockers, nestled the furnace room, and beside it hunkered the uniform-storage rooms, where row upon row of green wool military outfits dangled. The rooms contained enough uniforms to suit up every male student for the spring cadet march-past. Aiken's son and Moffat, another student, kibitzed inside the room, sorting uniforms, hanging the tunics and pants separately, and arranging them according to size. Aiken checked on them and left them to it.

Upstairs in the teacher's lounge, Aiken fidgeted alone, watching the news but rising every few minutes to twist the rabbit ears on the TV to improve reception. The screen suddenly jumped into unusual clarity. The announcer sat behind a desk at the Channel 7 newsroom. He said, "Soldiers from the 82nd and 101st Airborne will storm into the streets of Detroit shortly, rolling back the rioters, retaking the city, and reimposing civilization on the rioting black population." The screen flashed to shots of Selfridge Air Force Base and showed paratroopers boarding buses to transport them to the riot zone. After a few seconds of dead air time, the announcer concluded with, "The Airborne units include some coloured soldiers."

"So," Aiken said, "goddamn it to hell, there may be some good ones."

Miss Claire entered the lounge, and he rose and twisted the volume down as she closed on him. She passed over a cheque. "Two weeks of severance pay, Mr. Day. Your wife has been formally identified as someone involved in the Detroit unrest and apparently has been taken into custody. Consider yourself discharged from your position at Windsor Collegiate."

"A formal identification?" Aiken said. "You spoke to the hospital administrator?"

"I speak to whom I wish, and all my conversations remain privileged."

"I see," Aiken said.

"As indicated," Miss Claire said, "your position is terminated. You should exit the building promptly. The authorities remain within the reach of one phone call."

Miss Claire left the room. Aiken dialed the volume of the TV back up. The screen panned across body bags of dead soldiers from Vietnam, the bags being pulled from a transport plane at the Washington Dulles International Airport. The scene switched, cutting away to a demonstration at Berkeley with angry students chanting, "Hey! Hey! LBJ! How many kids did you kill today?" The Berkeley students torched an American flag, flames jumping upward, streaking, as if the flag had been drenched in gasoline. The reporter on the scene staggered backwards at the sight, at a loss for words. *That's a goddamn American flag they're burning.*

In the basement of the school, Aiken motioned to Adam and Moffat, who were still busy sorting uniforms. "New system this year," Aiken said. "No sorting of uniforms by size. Miss Claire prefers them in a pile, to allow students themselves to sort through them." He dragged a uniform from a hanger and flung it into the middle of the room. "Just pig-pen all the uniforms into a giant pile."

"Uniforms just make you like everyone else," Adam said. "That's my opinion."

"Cool. I get Miss Claire," Moffat said. "She wants to teach us buggers self-reliance."

Aiken nodded. "Exactly."

*   *   *

At home, Aiken hauled open the drawer containing the two rings; the gold circles were pressed together in the drawer with miscellaneous odds and ends: crayon bits, outdated keys, odd scraps of paper, assorted paperclips, and an old hairbrush. He studied his ring for a couple of minutes and then slipped it onto his finger. He pressed the drawer closed. *We'll go with the heart for a bit.* He hunted up the Canadian Club and splashed a shot over some ice cubes. *But just for a while, just till we get the lay of the land. Shit.* Lay of the land? *Maybe she's been laying someone else.*

*   *   *

At 3 p.m., Aiken seethed. In the living room, he was working on the bottle of Canadian Club, munching ice cubes to slow his drinking down as he viewed Berkeley students demonstrating against the war on the TV set; the sound of the set was turned down, the chants of the students muted. Adam came stomping into the room, and he slammed his fist against the wall. "What do you see?" he demanded. Aiken glanced up. His son stretched up before him, a strapping youth pushing toward the size of his grandfather Mayhem yet not up to his full growth. He possessed the same fierce blackness of his mother and grandfather, with pink palms and long fingers that could rifle a football or palm a basketball. Adam understood his father's look-over. "I am not goddamn Jackie Robinson," he said.

"A bit taller, I think."

"Funny."

"What do you see in the mirror?" Aiken asked his son.

"I get a freak looking back from every mirror," Adam said. "She was happy around me. No one fakes that every time, every day."

"Rachael?"

"You turned me into a freak."

"Oh yeah, that freak training. Cost us a damn fortune, but you were worth it."

"You made me into a white kid wearing black face."

"You been watching that Al Jolson movie again?" Aiken said.

"Not everything is a joke," Adam said.

"No, but the best goddamn things in life are. So tell me."

"You raised me like a white kid," Adam said. "You raised me like your own son."

"Yeah."

"I am black," Adam said, "You are white. I will always be black, and you will always be white."

An epiphany.

"People know me as the doofus black kid living on Victoria Avenue," Adam said, "going to Windsor Collegiate, and trying to date a white girl."

"We finally arrive at the issue."

"Rachael's dad," Adam said, "threatened to say shiva over her, unless she breaks off with me."

"*Shiva?*"

"The prayer for the dead. Kiss a nigger and go dead."

"This racism stuff makes you crazy," Aiken said. "It's been like that forever."

Aiken twisted back to the images on the TV. Angry white Berkeley students baited and battled angry white police officers.

"That's what you got?" Adam said. "That's all you got. No three parts to the guy: heart, brain, and python stuff?"

"You're thinking this stuff to death. It just makes you crazy."

Adam left the room, but he returned a few minutes later. Aiken glanced up. "My opinion, Pops," Adam said. "Not kissing someone might make you deader than kissing someone."

Aiken turned back to the TV. "Stop thinking so much, son." *You didn't ask, but yeah, these mixed-race love affairs seem to end poorly.*

*   *   *

Boris danced down the stairs wearing Aiken's navy blue blazer and grey flannel slacks. Adam was sitting on the living room couch, hands on knees, and Boris pulled up beside him.

"You didn't have an Afro earlier," Boris said.

"Earlier I had a pretty Jewish girlfriend," Adam said. "Now I have a perm and a new outlook. I may join the revolution."

"So, time to move on," Boris said.

"You really don't need no girlfriend," Adam said. "I mean, they're so afraid of gettin' pregnant they really don't do that much. If they French kiss you, it's like a big favour, like you should bow down, give thanks, and kiss their butts. They might as well wear concrete blouses for how hard it is to get those things tore off."

"You don't look like your dad," Boris said.

"Don't talk about my dad. He has his own sweats to deal with."

"There are strip shows in Detroit with real naked women," Boris said.

"White girls?" Adam said.

"Yeah, but mostly dark."

"There's a riot on."

"Some places are still open," Boris said.

"How much?" Adam said.

"Not much. You really had a Jewish girlfriend?"

"Yeah," Adam said, "and my mom knows Stokely Carmichael, and she met Malcolm X, and I don't have the girlfriend anymore."

"I can score some weed for us."

"Cool," Adam said, "and let's go to a strip club afterwards. I have forty dollars."

"I still have connections," Boris said.

"Cool, and then we'll see the strippers," Adam said. "But I don't have any ID."

"The forty dollars will scream out your name," said Boris. "We won't need ID."

*   *   *

Aiken picked up the receiver and said, "Hello." No answer. He let a few minutes tick by. Then, "Paris?" he said.

"I miss my kids and I miss you," she said, "and I wanted to make that clear to you."

"Where are you?"

"I'm being processed by the authorities," she said, "but I insisted on my phone call."

"Of course you did. Where are you?"

"I can take care of myself."

"Paris," he said, "your do-gooder instincts are working overtime. Slow down and come home."

"That's not going to happen for some time."

"Family is more important than anything," he said.

"The world is changing, and I'm part of it. This stuff started with those sit-ins down south and just grew. Things are changing."

"You should live with us," he said, "and watch your kids grow up."

"I feel guilty about that," she said, "every minute of every day."

"Come home."

"You learned about racism during the war."

"Sure," he said. "I understand. You have to fight a man like Hitler."

"Obviously," she said.

"And those sons of bitches who pushed people into the ovens."

"Yes, of course."

"And the truck driver who brought them to the camp, and the man who strung barbed wire around the camp."

"They're all as guilty as hell," she said.

"And the fellow who churned butter for the camp kitchen. And anyone working in a German munitions factory," he said. "Or the people in Omaha who didn't want to get involved in another European war and delayed their country's involvement."

"Not the same," said Paris. "The point is, things are different now."

"People are ordinary, and they don't change," Aiken said. "Everyone does good; everyone does bad. And everyone in the world does racism."

"Shut up."

"The long hair thins out," he said, "and hippies will bald up, just like their fathers did. The love beads will tarnish. Skeletons are remarkably similar, generation to generation."

"I understand what four years in a prison camp did to you," she said.

"I did four years in hell. I'm spent. Raising our children pushes me to the limit. They live in a racist world, and it will always be racist, and what I got for them is shooting hoops with Adam and hugging Sarah every chance I get."

"These young people are going to change the world."

"You must be on drugs."

"You do not know these young people."

"You think that I don't know young people," he said. "I am the functioning parent in this family. I meet with teachers, I help with schoolwork, and I tuck two kids in at night. I don't have time for Stokely

Carmichael meetings or shooting the shit with Martin Luther King, because I'm raising two kids."

"You can't stay stuck on Victoria Avenue," she said, "drinking green bottles of beer forever."

"I can. I can and I will."

"You park your butt next to the barbecue, with steaks grilling, sipping green beer, living the good life, but you don't actually do anything for civil rights. I am on the front lines."

"I goddamn well hug black kids on demand," he said. He slammed the phone down. *Bitch!*

Sarah came up behind him. "Phone call with Mom? Is she okay?"

"Yeah . . . no. We're okay, honey. Just married-people stuff. Not to worry."

"I need you here with me, Daddy," she said. "I'm going back to school with my friends, and they may be white, but they like me, and I don't need both of you in Detroit getting killed." She wrapped her arms around his waist. He hugged her back, pulling her in tight with his arms. *Shit, it's "Junior." It's goddamn Martin Luther King* Junior. *I forgot the Junior. I'm gonna be marked down for that mistake—probably get a letter from Lincoln himself, or maybe Ghandi, chucking me off the good-guys list.*

"Thank you, Daddy," Sarah said. She hugged him again, briefly squeezing him tight, and bounded up the stairs to her room.

Goddamn, I understand people. I understand people, young and old. How can she say that I don't understand young people?

*   *   *

Aiken's TV flipped to a scene recorded earlier in the day: a long-distance shot of US troopers unloading body bags from Vietnam at the Dulles International Airport. Solemn men in uniform were performing a necessary but gruesome task, seeking to impart the facade of military dignity to the brutal reality of combat death. Aiken parked on his couch, sitting upright, legs splayed, sipping whisky and munching ice cubes, not really focusing, just trying to stay relatively sober. He ignored the banging on the door for several minutes, but eventually he rose to find a young man with huge shoulders, a wild head of racy hair, and a scruffy beard standing alone on the porch. Aiken stepped outside and the door shut behind him.

Aiken said, "What?"

"Is Adam around?" the young man said.

"What?"

"Going to a concert," the fellow said. "Waiting for Adam. Dude, I'm Dixon."

"A concert?" Aiken said.

"Dude, don't you pick up on things fast."

"A concert for young people?" Aiken said.

"Exactly, dude," Dixon said. "I'm so damn glad you understand. It makes my whole day brighter."

Aiken tucked his shirt inside his trousers. "Maybe I'll go in his place," he said, "and see what young people are up to."

Dixon stepped back and held his hands up in front of him. "Whoa, dude." He backed down the porch steps.

Aiken reached in his pocket and pulled out a twenty-dollar bill. He held it up in front of him and then stepped forward and passed it over to Dixon. "To help with costs," he said. Dixon pocketed the money and shrugged, and Aiken followed him down the porch steps. *Goddamn, I still understand what a twenty-dollar bill says to a teenager.*

At the end of the walk, a dilapidated van, rust spots abounding, rested against the curb. "Must have broken down here," Aiken said. "Maybe he needs a tow." The horn from the van beeped twice.

"My wheels," Dixon said. They clambered into the van through the rear doors, and Dixon looped a leather strap about the handles to keep the back door shut before climbing over the seat into the front. A black girl peered over from the front passenger seat and waved to Aiken. Aiken smiled. The girl strung an arm around Dixon's neck as he climbed into the front seat. Inside the van, two wooden homemade benches ran along the walls. Two white girls were settled on the benches, one on each side.

Aiken sat down beside a stringy blonde girl dressed in a fringed leather jacket, who smiled at him. "Hey, man," she said, "I love you."

A smaller girl, opposite Aiken, wore a print dress that revealed a substantial, somewhat unrestrained, bosom. "I'm Janis," she said. "Love you, man."

Aiken said, "What?" *They love me? How much is this gonna cost, and will I need penicillin shots?*

Dixon cranked up the engine and rumbling consumed the vehicle, shaking and thumping the people inside. Black smoke slipped out through the hood, and the engine chugged. The van drifted away into light traffic. Janis poured liquid from a plastic container into a tumbler and offered it around. "Have some Kool-Aid for refreshment," she said. Everyone sipped Kool-Aid and passed the glass on to the next person.

The girl beside Aiken said, "I'm Bermuda—warm and bumpy like the island, only not as bumpy as Janis." Janis smiled at Aiken. Her cleavage rippled with the motion of the vehicle, and Aiken turned away to face Bermuda. *Oh my God. Isn't there some sort of government program to provide her with a bra? Maybe a welfare program for big-bosom types—"re-engineering drain culverts for personal use" or something?*

"What do you do, man?" Janis said to Aiken. "You seem, um . . . you know . . . older, and sort of straight." She reached out and pulled Aiken's shirt from his pants and undid his top two buttons. She folded his shirtsleeves back. "Better," she said.

"History teacher," Aiken said. "Between assignments right now." *Keep your eyes on the small-bosomed girl, little-boobs Bermuda—less likely to offend.*

"Cool," Bermuda said. She slipped the plastic cup into his hand when it came back round to her. "More Kool-Aid?" she said. Aiken sipped.

"Is this van stolen?" Aiken said. "I need to know that." The Kool-Aid tumbler tripped around the van for a third time. Everyone sipped.

Dixon called back, "Does it really matter, dude?"

"Damn warm today," Aiken said. "Did we just scoot by Jackson Park?"

"We're travelling a little farther," Janis said, "Going to see Joplin."

"Joplin?" Aiken said. "Joplin, Missouri, in this vehicle?" Everyone laughed or giggled. *I've always been fairly witty.*

Aiken said to Bermuda, "This cup is weird. I swear it's moving, twisting about in your hand, almost alive."

"Yeah, man," Bermuda said. "It's dancing. Don't you love it?"

Aiken had a niggling thought. "Does *what* matter, Dixon?"

The van rumbled along for 30 minutes, everyone sipping Kool-Aid along the way, while the van rocked back and forth in soothing fashion. They ended up at a field, and Dixon spun the van in beside a few other vehicles, mostly older trucks or beat-up vans, some with Confederate flags draped across the back window.

"Not many Cadillacs or Lincolns," Aiken said. "Where do those fellas park?" Everyone tumbled out of the van and stood together, feeling bonded, and considered the scene spread out before them. "Man . . ." Aiken said. "Man, check out the grass. It's so damn inviting." He stepped out of his shoes and peeled off his socks. "I never, ever set my toes in grass so vividly green."

Bermuda put her arm through Aiken's arm. They sauntered away from the others, and she leaned her head on his shoulder. Two bearded fellows, possibly Jesus and a young Karl Marx, passed by them. Karl waved a peace sign at them, and Bermuda returned the gesture. She reached into her jacket pocket and pushed a crumpled, bedraggled, hand-rolled cigarette at Aiken. He accepted in and set it out in the palm of his hand. "What do I do with this?" he said, passing it back to her.

"This is good shit," she said. She slicked up the joint, rolling it between her lips, and flamed it with a wooden match struck on her jacket zipper. Cheeks puffing in and out, she demonstrated. "Just fill your lungs," she said, squeaking out the words. Aiken followed suit. "We can stop the war," Bermuda said.

Aiken didn't reply, but he reflected on her comment. After a few puffs sucked into his lungs, he thought, *Well sure, if we get everyone smoking this shit.*

Bermuda sucked on the joint again. "There have been four serious attempts to change the Western world," she said.

"Oh, wow." Aiken said. *The printing press, the flush toilet, Old Spice aftershave—and what? And what?*

"Three of the revolutions," Bermuda said, "the French, the Russian, and the American, were true only in the beginning. Just true in the beginning, man."

"True?"

"True to the people, you know . . . Afterwards, they forgot their roots, man, and the revolutions went off the track. They turned into huge bureaucracies and administrations."

Aiken had another toke. "Flush toilets work damn good; I grew up with an outhouse. Damn cold crapping in January, when the mercury hits minus 40."

"Only the Cuban Revolution is different," Bermuda said. "Castro keeps true to the people. He keeps things simple and pure. He even sends Che Guevara to help the countries in South America join the revolution." She put a hand on Aiken's chest. "Do you know about Che, man?" Aiken nodded. "Oh, yeah, for sure." *The guy who posed for all those T-shirts?*

Bermuda slipped even closer to Aiken. She threw an arm about his neck and pointed to the young people heading toward the music stage. "These people could stop the war," she said. He nodded and toked again. *But is anyone smoking this shit really gonna try?* She beckoned with a finger and led him away from the bandstand, far enough away that the music sounds faded and slipped into background. Bermuda led him to a park bench to view the concert from a distance. Aiken said, "Mellow is how I feel right now. I feel in perfect tune with the world right now."

"It *is* good shit," Bermuda said. "*Really* good shit."

"Check out the leaves on that tree."

"In the eye of my mind," Bermuda said, "I imagine what the world could be." Together they rolled off the bench and flopped onto the grass. He noticed her ass for the first time. *Perky little thing.*

"Mm, nice," Aiken said, pitching onto his back. "My wife's is black."

"I imagine a world," Bermuda said, "where no one goes hungry."

"Nah," Aiken said. "It's a red maple. We had one at home."

"Women and blacks are oppressed," Bermuda said. "No decent jobs for them in Detroit. Especially after this riot. People are good, man. The form of government oppresses them."

"Cool."

"Surely you see the failings of the system. Inequality, injustice, unfairness, and exploitation—"

"I once met a girl with a harelip."

"What?"

"Where do you learn this stuff?" Aiken said.

"University of Michigan. I signed the Manifesto."

"The manifesto?"

"The SDS Manifesto."

"The SDS?"

"Students for a Democratic Society, man," Bermuda said.

"Remind me about the manifesto," Aiken said.

"The country needs participatory democracy—which means no bureaucracy and no administration." Aiken thought about that. *So, 150 million people getting together over coffee to set traffic speed limits for Kalamazoo?* "It hangs together in a weird sort of way," he said. *Probably need more good shit to fully appreciate it.*

He sat up. "Did you ever go on any of those sit-ins in Georgia, or ride the freedom buses?"

"My father threatened to cut off my money if I went," Bermuda said. "But I was there in spirit." *Not quite the Rosa Parks get-it-done stuff.*

They moved back closer to the concert stage. Bermuda wandered off, and Aiken plopped down beside Dixon. "Dude. Your generation has gotta get things straight," Dixon said. "People are just not about war. Love is far more important."

"Did you ever go on any of those sit-ins in Georgia?" Aiken said. "Or ride the freedom buses?"

"Why would I do that? You could get your ass busted doing that. The KKK has serious problems with people who do that."

"So, what do you believe in?" Aiken said.

Dixon pulled him close and whispered. "Love."

"Love?"

"You gotta say *love*, dude," Dixon said. "It goes over better than asking straight out for sex or admitting that you only want to pork her."

Pork her?

"These are the times to stay in school forever, dude," Dixon said. "University girls have access to birth control pills now, and they ain't afraid to ball a groovy guy."

"Really?"

"So, do whatever you have to do," Dixon said. "Stop showering if it works, or stop using a barber if it plays well with the babes. Dress in weird flowered shirts if you have to, but get them into the sack. Someday these young broads are gonna realize what Helen of Troy always knew."

"What is that?"

"That babes got a monopoly on it, so why give it away? Free love is an unbelievable gift for guys. And right now, there is some damn good female flesh available, just for the asking."

"Wow." *Free porking.*

"When that stuff goes south . . ." Dixon said, "I really don't know, dude." He shrugged. "Maybe become a lawyer and make the big dough. Go after the big bucks. Get a wife with big tits, someone to give you a good ride."

They sat in silence. The crowds increased around the stage; the concert murmur increased. "But above all," Dixon said, "keep good drug connections throughout your whole life, so you can buy in bulk, cut it up, and resell it to friends. That way you smoke for free." *A rather vicious rejection of capitalism.*

"So, what about this war in Vietnam?" Aiken said.

"Dude," Dixon said, "they're killing people over there in gobs. You might get a leg shot off. I wouldn't go. Rather go to prison and be raped by big black guys. Play the percentages—try to get into law school."

As the time for the main act approached and the warm-up acts finished off, streams of people shifted toward the stage, fusing in, drifting slowly toward the bandstand, joining other young people.

Drug transactions abounded. When Aiken's group approached the edge of the crowd, they tumbled down on the grass. People swayed and rocked back and forth with others. A woman singer stumbled to the centre of the stage and wrapped her hands around the microphone.

Bermuda said, "The other Janis. Just listen to her."

The wailing into the microphone began, and the crowd quieted at once.

"Holy shit," Aiken said. "The tonsils on that gal."

After the concert, they made their way back to the van. Janis left the group, attaching herself to a stocky fellow in a tie-dyed shirt.

"Each concert is so unique," Bermuda said, nestling in beside Aiken. "Sometimes you float above people, sensing each one. Sometimes you morph into something else, maybe a flower. Sometimes your karma changes. Man! The far Eastern religions get it right."

"Groovy," said a tall scraggly fellow who had joined their group.

The black girl said, "Dylan met the Maharishi, and both swam naked in the Ganges River."

"Dylan Thomas?" Bermuda said.

"Or did you mean Bob Dylan?" Dixon said.

"Or maybe Marshal Dillon?" Aiken said. Much laughter ensued. *Probably not the marshal.*

The black girl sitting up front beside Dixon dropped her arm from around him and turned to face Aiken. "Haven't seen you for a while," she said. "Where's the black do-gooder wife these days?"

"Have we met?" Aiken said.

"I'm Linda. You know, sugar—from the unit." *Of course you are. Why didn't I recognize you? And where in hell are my shoes and socks?*

*　　*　　*

At 6 p.m., Aiken knocked on the door and brushed through the empty waiting room into Dr. Sam's office. Dr. Sam hunched over his desk, puzzling over an ink blot. He was twisting it from side to side, first this way and then that. "Shit," Dr. Sam said, "A penis. Shit, shit, shit. It's *always* a damn penis."

Dr. Sam held up a finger, the sign for Aiken to wait a second. He set the ink blot aside and drew Aiken's file from the desk drawer, quickly flipping pages about, reviewing his notes. He swung his head up from the file. "Do you ever have the urge to fart, Mr. Day?" he said.

"Farting? I'm here for therapy."

"So, I repeat the question," Dr. Sam said. "Do you ever have the urge to fart?"

"No sir," Aiken said, "not, generally. I either fart or I don't fart. I make no conscious decisions about farting. Just so you understand—animal reactions only."

Dr. Sam stared at Aiken for a few seconds, "But it must be accurate to say, Mr. Day, that you repress some urges?"

"I guess I do have urges that I repress." *And urges to repress other urges.*

Dr. Sam said, "And the urge to kill, Mr. Day—did the urge to kill ever seep into you? Please be honest with me."

You must think I'm the village idiot. "No, never the urge to kill."

"You must understand, Mr. Day, that the true evil in the world begins with what people repress."

Farts are the enemy? And here we spent the war trying to kill Hitler.

Dr. Sam smiled. "Ask yourself this: what part of your inner self lusted to marry a black woman? What part, Mr. Day?"

"Ah, the part that knocked her up?"

"That part doesn't actually think so much," Dr. Sam said. He pulled out a sheet of paper, wrote a note, and then closed the file.

"Wait," Aiken said. "Maybe I loved her. Maybe my damn heart was stepping up to the plate." Dr. Sam smiled politely. "Why didn't I think of that," Aiken said. "It's a much better answer."

"I've closed my file up," Dr. Sam said. "See you next time, Mr. Day."

Aiken did not move. Dr. Sam looked at his watch. Finally he said, "Well, we have a few minutes, Mr. Day. Tell me about the concentration camp. Do you ever think about the horrors of war?"

Aiken touched his forehead and felt dryness. "Well, I figured out the first horror of the war."

"Tell me, Mr. Day."

"The Jews," Aiken said. "Krauts deciding based on race to burn some folks and not others."

Dr. Sam nodded. "Yes, good, good—the Jews," he said. "And what do you view as the second horror of the war?"

"Well, that I can't say who did it," Aiken said.

"No?" Dr. Sam said. "But we can easily pin the blame on Hitler and those Nazi thugs for the bad stuff."

A small tremor swept through Aiken. "Probably why I don't think about it," he said.

"I find that once we verbalize a problem," Dr. Sam said, "the solution becomes obvious."

"You possess a rare gift for the obvious," Aiken said.

Dr. Sam spun the chair around until he rested beside Aiken. "One always appreciates a compliment, Mr. Day."

Aiken nodded.

Friday, July 28, 1967

At 9 a.m. a single candle flickered in the basement of Victoria Avenue, spinning off scant, irregular light that reflected off the stone walls, nibbling along the rock curves and dripping shadows and dark goblin spots. Aiken sat on a firm wooden kitchen chair, the sort of spindle-back chair any man possessing calloused hands and a wood lathe would have cranked out easily, years ago. It was the sort of chair no longer in demand for fancy veneer kitchens, the sort of chair that slammed against a man's back firmly—a no-bullshit, Division Road-farmer sort of chair that paid little homage to fad or fashion.

The stiff chair back conveyed unusual comfort to Aiken this morning, reinforcement even, given the fevers chopping at his brain. Aiken's elbows jabbed onto the square, scuffed oaken table, and he sliced off a piece of cheese with a Buck knife every so often, separating each slice from a sizable block of cheddar. He chewed on each piece slowly, munching instinctively, mechanically, and taking occasional short sips from a bottle of red wine, already half done. A day's growth of beard brushed his face, and beads of sweat dribbled down his cheeks. Every few minutes he spun his fingers against his right temple, reached down, and wiped damp fingers against his trousers without realizing it.

The stairs squeaked as Mayhem banged the timber treads on his way down, followed by Sarah. Reaching the last tread, Mayhem said, "Nice hideout."

"Apparently not good enough," Aiken said.

Mayhem smiled, cheeks splitting, teeth shining, black face lively for a few seconds. He spun a chair around with a few fingers, without apparent effort, and draped his body over it. "I called the psych ward," he said. "No one is saying where Paris has been transferred to, and my contact there has been let go."

They canned the Black Janitor.

Moffat hollered down the stairs, "Coming down at ya, Mr. D."

"You invited a whole passel of folk?" Aiken said. Several students from 11A trooped down the stairs behind Moffat. To the students, he said, "I am no longer your history teacher." *So piss off, boys and girls. I am in full-blown-fever and drinking mode.* He sliced off a piece of cheese and chewed. Mayhem unfolded a few card-table chairs, and the students scuffled about and settled in, some seated but most standing, leaning against the basement walls. Aiken sipped from the bottle.

One of the students, Diane, broke the silence. "We support your wife, Mr. Day."

"You support my wife?" Aiken said. Diane nodded. *Nothing a firm bra wouldn't do, and I wouldn't have to mark its goddamn history test.*

Moffat stepped forward. "Cool. This basement setting," he said. "It's perfect for espionage, or criminal activity. Classic, Mr. D, absolutely classic. It just screams out: Fruit Cellar Felon."

"Thank you, Moffat," said Aiken. *Every class needs a clown.*

"Detroit turned into a ghetto without anybody realizing it," a student said. *A few people might have realized it. Maybe those not eating three squares a day.*

"Detroit is burning for a reason," the same student said, "and we understand that now."

Aiken sipped. "Thank you."

"On the radio talk shows," said the student, whose name was Aaron, "all the phone-ins focus on Paris Day."

Aiken slit the cheese block again and said, "What do they say?"

"That she joined the Black Panthers," Aaron said. "Everyone agrees on that point."

"I don't agree," Mayhem said. "That's a load of malarkey."

Aiken slipped the piece of cheese into his mouth and said, "What else do these clever people say?"

"That she disappeared into the underground," Aaron said, "and is fighting for black liberation with Stokely Carmichael and other radicals."

"Paris in the underground?" Mayhem said. "More malarkey. I know my own daughter."

"Paris goes her own way," Aiken said. "She might be doing the things they say."

Mayhem draped a hand on Aiken's shoulder and put his mouth close to Aiken's ear. "Bullshit," he whispered. "That damn Administrator fellow is crapping in your home, and you're lapping it up. Don't believe the stuff he's putting out to the press."

"Maybe it's his doing," Aiken said, "but maybe not."

"No one else but him threw this Black Panther crap out to the public," Mayhem said. "No one else but him could have talked people into calling radio stations, saying stuff about Paris, to confuse things, to throw us off." Aiken sliced off another piece of cheese. Mayhem drew his hand back and pointed a finger. "You spoke vows to each other, Aiken."

Aiken said. "Both of us spoke vows."

"I get it," Mayhem said. "You think she let you down. So what is this, the Aiken Day two-wrongs-make-a-right theory?"

"Might be," Aiken said.

"You know this Administrator fellow," Mayhem said. "Tell me. Where is he gonna hide Paris? Where should I go look for her?"

"Not anywhere on Victoria Avenue," Aiken said, "for damn sure. She'd be having an allergic reaction, maybe break out in a white rash from the good life."

"Damn cute," Mayhem said. "So where do I hunt for her? In jail?"

"The jail gives a phone call," Aiken said, "and those jail guard fellas don't work for the Administrator."

"So he stuffs her in some sort of nursing home?" Mayhem said. "With nurses on duty and a doctor to patch up cuts and stuff."

"Nursing homes count the bodies after the patients die," Aiken said. "They report things to the government. The Administrator needs to keep her out of the way, in a place where nothing appears out of the ordinary."

"Give me some more," Mayhem said.

"Paris chose her life," Aiken said. "Saving the goddamn world—that's her plan. My plan—my only plan—is grilling steaks on Victoria Avenue and raising two kids. So send me to hell."

Sarah stepped up beside Aiken and placed her hand against his cheek. "Do you miss Mom?" she said. Aiken stretched out his arms out and Sarah rolled into them. *Shit. Someone always plays the love card.*

"Don't you miss Mom a bit?" she said.

Aiken pushed the bottle to the side. "I do, honey," Aiken said. "I miss the sass she dropped into my life every single day we spent together."

"I'm glad, Daddy." Sarah kissed Aiken on the cheek. "So help find Mom." *Yeah. Brain, maybe you should take a brief vacation. Take two aspirin and sit on the bench. Someone just smacked a line drive up the middle of the heart.*

Mayhem rose up and squared his shoulders away. After a few seconds, the students of 11A rose as well. No one spoke, but everyone looked to Aiken.

Shit, I know where she is. "We might need some help," Aiken said.

"We can help," Aaron said. "The students of 11A will pitch in."

"High-school students?" Mayhem said.

"You might wish for John Wayne," Moffat said, "but sometimes Bob Hope is the only guy with a horse and a gun." *Moffat, you are the single reason they don't issue firearms to high-school teachers.*

Aiken punched the cork back into the bottle. "The Administrator is in control of the unit and misdirecting people about her whereabouts. Paris is back on the unit," Aiken said. "She's back on the eighth floor. Never left. No one checks on nutcases."

Aiken stood up but turned away. "What else?" Mayhem said.

"He has access to those damn electro-shock experiments."

*   *   *

Aiken found Honey sitting on the living room floor in her fancy black underwear, surrounded by shoes. Shoes covered the entire living room floor. "A woman only needs one pair of shoes for an outfit," she said. "But God, you've got to get it just right."

"What's going on?" Aiken said.

Honey laughed. "I had a few tokes to help me choose the proper shoes," she said.

"A few tokes?"

"You know," Honey said. She put her fingers to her lips and made a *thwippp* sound. "A few . . . tokes."

"Sure," Aiken said, "a few tokes."

"A damn disaster," she said. "Smoke some pot, choose a shoe. Could anything be easier?"

"So, what happened?"

Honey began to weep. "Every shoe is beautiful in its own right. Every shoe needs to be chosen. Every shoe is equal."

"Shit," Aiken said.

"Shoes are inherently equal," said Honey. "Who am I? I have no right to choose one shoe over another." She put her hands to her face.

"Do you need some meds," Aiken said.

"I need more feet. I need a foot for every shoe. I was born handicapped, unequal to the task at hand. The revolution will pass me by. I am a lousy Marxist-Leninist."

Boris came into the room from the back porch. The blue sports coat was shredded and the grey flannel pants stained and torn. His hair was astray. "Yeth, it wath a hell of a party," he said. "Where am I?"

"Let me give Dr. Sam a call," Aiken said. *Victoria Avenue chews up and spits out two more, shipping them back to crazy.*

*   *   *

Aiken and Mayhem hunched beside one another on the back-porch steps of Victoria Avenue. Adam slept nearby on the wicker lounge, still dead to the world after his outing with Boris.

"Just give me the plan," Mayhem said sharply. Aiken brushed by him into the house and poured out two fingers of Canadian Club into a glass for each of them. Mayhem cupped his and sipped. "Sorry," Mayhem said. "I'm just jumpy. Let's start the damn thing. I feel like a pinch hitter with the game on the line."

"Start phoning people," Aiken said. "We meet up at the Holiday Inn within the hour. It would be good to drum up a few black folk, but we welcome anyone with a modern outlook or a loud voice." Mayhem nodded. When Aiken had finished his Canadian Club and munched the ice cubes into oblivion, he phoned and booked the Holiday Inn's Conference Room A, on the ground level. Mayhem took over the phone and began calling friends.

The Holiday Inn actually suited the group of rebels quite well. In an age when most cities demanded construction using cold steel and hard concrete for multi-storeyed buildings, the Holiday Inn had extracted minor concessions from the City of Windsor. They built the hotel using wood, a type of construction marginally out of municipal favour because of the rampant risk of fire. But with a building perched on the banks of the Detroit River, so the argument ran, a bucket brigade promptly formed to fight any fire in the building could prove very effective.

Aiken's first drink on Victoria Avenue had eased the sweats somewhat, so he adopted one of his pa's other dictums: not the-three-parts-of-the-male-body one, the never-be-drunk-but-never-be-entirely-sober one. He transported a few pints of liquor to the Holiday Inn, as a fever fighter, just in case the need arose. As the hours wore on there, even with an occasional shot of booze the sweats crept back. They were gradual at the start—nothing but an occasional drop on his forehead for the first hour or so—but always close to the surface.

Mayhem, familiar with the fire department's ongoing concerns about the incendiary nature of the

Holiday Inn, approached a hippie in what became a recurring theme. "Put out the damn cigarette," Mayhem said.

"*Thwippp.* This ain't no damn cigarette, man."

Moffat pushed through the doors of Conference Room A, where he bumped into Mayhem and Aiken. "Why collect at the Holiday Inn?" Mayhem said. "It's the largest hotel in Windsor, totally exposed, sitting on the river just spitting distance from Detroit. There is no sense to this."

"Beg to differ, Reverend Chase," Moffat said. "It is so cool. The most successful guerilla raid in history involved hiding out in the open, up the butt of a wooden horse, and a wooden hotel is almost the same as a wooden horse."

"The same as a horse?" Mayhem said.

One of the hippies overheard. "You got 'horse,' man?" The man moved toward Mayhem, rolling up a sleeve. "You got some 'horse'?"

Mayhem elbowed the man aside. "Move on," Mayhem said. "Or watch some hippie ass get whupped." The man drifted away.

"Brutal," Moffat said, "but cool. Totally necessary, Reverend C."

To Aiken, Mayhem said, "Do something about the people showing up here. Drugged-up hippies are no damn help."

"For now," Aiken said, "we wait. We wait for a few more people and just a bit more time."

A row of tables backed the east wall of Conference Room A, with unopened wine bottles resting on the tables. The bottles were pushed together without order, mostly dry reds but one or two bottles of Chablis. Aiken Day slowly made his way down the table, using a sommelier's corkscrew to mechanically yank up cork after cork; he carefully set the cork beside each bottle. The perfunctory effort drew a tad of warmth but still only the occasional drop of sweat. When he reached the end of the table, he pulled another shot of Canadian Club. Someone whispered to him, "I heard they got some horse."

Mayhem came up beside Aiken. "Let the wine go, Aiken, and get on with it. We don't need more liquor at this outing."

"We do, actually," Aiken said. "We need to bring out the rabble-rousing nature of people." *We are gonna need* un-*repression. We need hundreds of people farting up a storm. We need a big-time, old-fashioned, furious, fart storm.*

Mayhem crossed to the centre of the room, balanced behind the small podium, and began to tap the microphone, saying, "One, two, three," to see whether the audio worked and people could hear him. The room measured 12 foot by 20 foot, so people heard.

A hippie type said, "Groovy, man."

Mayhem said to Aiken, "We've picked up enough people to storm a dozen hospitals, so let's dump these hippies." One of the hippies approached with a smelly cigarette, and Mayhem dragged the butt from his hand and ground it into the floor. "Why don't you go rob a bank, buster?" he said. "In Texas."

Then he said, "We've gathered enough people. Let's roll on to the hospital and demand her release, force the issue if necessary."

"Push the alcohol," Aiken said.

"Drugs are driving these hippie engines," Mayhem said. "I wouldn't let these people puke in the trunk of my car."

A man with long hair and a beaded shirt approached Mayhem. "Whoa, man, count me in for that." Mayhem started toward him.

"Hold up," Aiken said.

Mayhem stopped. "We do not need damn hippies to help us out."

"We need them," Aiken said. "And we need some radical, ass-kicking slogans as well."

"Like what?" Mayhem said.

"Like Black Power, or Leave Vietnam Now or, my personal favourite, Hey, Hey, LBJ—How Many Kids Did You Kill Today? We need stuff for the press and TV cameras to focus on."

"What in hell will people watching TV think?" Mayhem said.

"They'll be pissed off that 'I Love Lucy' is delayed."

"Stop the damn war," yelled Moffat. People nodded.

"Get the hell out of Vietnam," someone called back. People nodded. There were more shouts. "Pass out some more liquor," Aiken said. "And get your black folk riled up. They look too damn civilized. Why are they wearing neckties?"

One hour later, Mayhem pulled Aiken aside and dragged him outside to the Dodge, where he popped up the trunk to reveal a folded-over blanket. Mayhem pulled the corner aside, just enough, and Aiken knew instantly what lay under the cover.

"You buried a .303 rifle under that blanket," Aiken said.

"The old army standby," Mayhem said. "I felt you should know, Aiken. This weapon comes with us, and we ain't leaving without her."

We ain't leaving without her? Aiken said, "'Her' being Paris, or 'her' being the .303?"

"Paris is the future," Mayhem said. "A black university professor at a white university, living with a white history teacher and raising black kids in a white neighbourhood, and—"

"'Living with'?" Aiken said. "You mean 'married to.' Married to. We were married in your damn house, and there was a shotgun leaning against the wall in case anyone wanted to argue."

"Right. Sorry," Mayhem said. "Married to. Yeah, yeah, married to."

"And the black Lab dog," Aiken said.

"Yeah, and married to the damn dog, if you want." Mayhem smoothed the blanket and said, "Will this put us in hell, Aiken? That's okay by me, but are we crazy for doing this?"

"Absolutely not," Aiken said. *And if I am wrong, we can repress this shit and get pills. I can help you with that.* Aiken rubbed his hand over the weapon under the blanket and said, "We are not leaving without her."

"Okay."

"'Her' being Paris," Aiken said, "just so we are clear on that. 'Her' is Paris, not the .303."

"Yeah. Tell me the plan," Mayhem said.

"The first thing we do . . ."

"Yes."

"You pop inside the Holiday Inn, and you pull the fire-alarm bell."

"I pull the fire-alarm bell?" Mayhem said. "What for?"

"So no one burns to death," Aiken said.

"Yes, good—" Mayhem said. "So no one burns to death! Why would anyone burn to death?"

"Because of one of the other things you are going to do."

"What?" Mayhem said. "What did you say, Aiken?"

"We start our own race riot. We wait for TV cameras, and then we burn down the Holiday Inn."

"We burn down the Holiday Inn." After a few seconds, he said, "We burn down the Holiday Inn?"

"I am so glad we agree," Aiken said. *That's a goddamn relief.* Aiken jerked a pint bottle of Canadian Club from his back pocket and held it out. "Slug down a bit of some old-fashioned fart juice." *There is no substitute on earth for fart juice.*

"Fart juice?" said Mayhem. "Sure, call it what you will. Yeah, I might just have a sip." "Gimme some damn fart juice, for sure." He wrestled the bottle away and pumped a few shots down his throat. He wiped a hand across his lips. "Who builds a goddamn hotel out of wood?" Mayhem said. "Only idiots do that."

"Exactly," Aiken said. "Those goddamn Greeks up to mischief again."

Windsor Hospital

At 3 p.m., Aiken Day and Mayhem Chase dumped the Dodge at the curb on Ouellette Avenue directly across from Windsor Hospital. Mayhem unlocked the trunk and lifted the lid. Aiken pushed the Canadian Club toward him, but Mayhem batted it away. "What in hell are we doing?" Mayhem said.

Aiken swallowed a full measure and returned the flask to his pocket. "Dealing with the same old shit, Mayhem," Aiken said, "since forever."

"When do we jump off?" Mayhem said. Aiken smiled but made no reply.

*   *   *

It was 8 p.m., and eight floors above Aiken and Mayhem, in the psych ward, Boris sauntered up to the windows of his room. Black smoke was spiralling above the Holiday Inn, clearly visible. Honey sat on the bed, legs crossed.

"My God, the hotel ith burning!" shouted Boris.

"Dr. Sam said to be quiet and keep out of sight," Honey said.

Boris ran out of the room and shouted again, "The hotel ith burning!"

He prepared to cry out again, but so many patients raced to the lounge that he held back, while people jostled, seeking the best view. The sirens began then, screaming out their message, and police cars raced down Ouellette Avenue toward the river.

In an empty room down the corridor, Dr. Sam glanced down at the scene and sipped from a small bottle of Crown Royal whiskey. "I shouldn't have helped the Administrator with Mrs. Day," he said. He sipped again.

On the street below, as the first police car wailed by him, Aiken smiled and held out a thumbs-up. Mayhem smiled back. Aiken removed a blue bandana from the trunk, wiped at the sweat on his brow and tied the cloth around his head. He handed a red cloth to Mayhem, who tied it around his forehead. Aiken dragged the .303 from the trunk and unwrapped the blanket from the weapon.

"Yeah, fighting the same old stuff," Mayhem said. "Stuff that never ends, stuff that never seems to go away."

On the eighth floor, watching the smoke twist above the Holiday Inn, Boris said, "Thit, thit!"

The Fat Man laughed, snorting through his nose. "*Thit, thit?*" he said. "What a faggy thing to say. My goodness, my good man. Thit, thit?" The Fat Man doubled over in laughter. "Thit, thit, thit. Ha!" Honey laughed as well, bending over, holding her sides, and wheezing. The fire from the burning Holiday Inn leaped out dramatically, crimson hues spreading across the Windsor skyline and orange reflections bouncing across the Detroit River. All this was clearly visible to the patients in the psych ward who pressed against the windows. There were 24 patients gathered about the windows, pushing or nudging each other, all anxious, all staring out at the burning hotel. Sirens blared.

The Fat Man rubbed his finger alongside his nose. "A hotel fire screams money," he said, "and we all know who owns the hotels."

The Minister rubbed a finger along his nose in similar fashion, nodding. "The Jew media is already on the scene, throwing out cover-up right now, making it look like the Frogs or the Polacks did it."

The Fat Man nodded and lowered his voice. "Jewish lightning, for goddamn certain."

The blaze mesmerized most patients. Honey began to weep. After a few minutes, the Minister wrapped his arm around the shoulders of the Fat Man and whispered more comments about the worldwide Jewish conspiracy. The Shift Attendant took note and called over, "Do you two homos need a room together?" They jumped apart. Honey screamed with laughter at the two men.

Aiken Day, hell-bent on his mission, rolled down the eighth floor hallway toward the psych ward, with his father-in-law stepping beside him, stride for stride. Mayhem Chase, an imposing figure by any standard because of the width of his shoulders, now coupled this stature with a fierce, raging blackness. His heart and spirit torched up, he was a veritable giant as he charged toward the ward, with the red bandana tucked around his forehead and the .303 rifle cradled across his left arm. Reaching the unit doors, Aiken paused and smiled, nodding to Mayhem, who raised his foot and kicked at the two doors, swatting them open. When the doors clanged open and the echoes finished bouncing through the unit, a hush settled over the eighth floor.

Aiken and Mayhem crossed into the lounge, making straight to the windows. Patients and staff backed away, pushing against the walls to make space for the two men. Aiken and Mayhem stopped at the windows and surveyed the city, taking note of the smoke plumes rising from the Holiday Inn. Flames sparked up on the top floor.

"The doing of radicals," Aiken said.

"That damn Stokely fellow again," Mayhem said.

"People farting about and failing to repress," Aiken said. "No sense to it. Give them over to medication, I say."

Honey stole up beside Aiken, reached up, and pulled the bandana from his forehead. She wiped his brow and held the cloth out for him to see. The cloth showed damp, very damp. "Feels like the furnace started up," Aiken said.

Honey tapped his cheek. "Look at my eyes, Aiken. You are heating up. What colour are my eyes?"

"What?" Aiken said. "Your eyes are good—normal colour. Doing fine here. Stop your worry."

Honey said, "Normal colour? Red? Are they red, Aiken?"

"Well—"

She dropped to the floor and began to cry.

Aiken and Mayhem paused outside of the lounge, sharing sips of Canadian Club from the flask while they took stock of the eighth floor. Rivulets of sweat poured down Aiken's face.

"Move the patients into the cafeteria," Mayhem said. "We can keep a better eye on them."

The Fat Man tapped Boris on the shoulder. "Come on, fag. Let's move into the cafeteria. All cats are grey in the dark."

"Right," Aiken said, his words slurring. "This begins it—always. First, separate people into groups, specific categories, just like Stalag 8B."

"Slow down," Mayhem said.

"In Stalag 8B, I was assigned to the Canadian compound." Mayhem placed a hand on Aiken's shoulder. "Hey you, Boris," Aiken said, "start up a queer compound."

"He's not homosexual," Mayhem said.

"Silly preacher man," Aiken said. "Never let facts get in the way of categorizing people. It's a telltale sign of repression."

"Sit down for a second," Mayhem said.

"We need consistency and predictability," Aiken said, "and a sense of proper placement. We need these things before we can mold the world into what we know it can be."

"Aiken, park it here," Mayhem said, patting a couch and smiling up at him. "Rest up a bit." Aiken brushed him off. "Damn!" Mayhem said. "There are more people here than I figured."

"Shoot a few down like cur dogs," Aiken said, wiping his forehead. "We'll need a cur dog compound."

Honey said, "Please, Aiken, sit down here." He ignored her request, setting a hand on her shoulder and whispering into her ear, "On the beach at Dieppe, when the shooting slowed and everyone lay dead or dying, before the Germans pitched down from the headlands, we collected ammunition from our dead. I mean, what the hell does a dead man need ammo for? A dead man shoots no gun. He doesn't hate or kill, so steal whatever you want from a dead man. He just don't damn well care anymore."

"But you weren't dead, Aiken?" Honey said.

"Really," Aiken said. He turned to Mayhem. "Christ, we'll need a dead soldier compound."

"Aiken, go park your butt somewhere," Mayhem said, "out of the way."

The remaining staff and patients collected in the cafeteria, moving quickly, following Mayhem's gestures.

"Somehow," Mayhem said, "we gotta keep these people in the cafeteria while we search for Paris."

Aiken felt the sweats increase and bubble against his brain. He said to Mayhem, "Stand outside, so the nutbars can see you through the glass." Mayhem nodded. When the cafeteria doors closed behind him, Aiken addressed the patients and staff in slow measured tones, voice steely calm. He wiped a hand across his face, felt the dampness, and bent his head, glancing at the ground for a few seconds. Then he raised his eyes slowly until he stared eyeball to eyeball with the patients in front of him. "Any goddamn man stepping outside these doors during the next 60 minutes will be raped to death by the big black man you see through the glass. This man is an escaped convict from Jackson State Prison who has venereal disease. His pecker drips poison." Silence fell over the room, blanketing the patients. After a few seconds, one man gagged; another man whimpered. Aiken paused for the room to digest that information and quiet somewhat before he continued. "And any woman who steps outside," said Aiken, the women suddenly quiet, "won't be raped."

Aiken went outside through the doors to Mayhem, sweat pissing down his forehead. "I've constructed the perfect white hell for those people," he said. "It just came to me all of a sudden." He spun about suddenly and yelled back into the cafeteria. "And turn down the goddamn thermostat."

Aiken and Mayhem bounded down the halls, flinging doors open as they went, and headed toward the lock-down room where the staff administered the shock treatments. They rounded a corner and found Paris sitting in a chair by herself. She waited with her hands folded in her lap, dressed in civvies; a crisp white blouse with a navy skirt was tucked demurely about her knees.

Paris smiled at Aiken. "Am I free to leave now?" she said.

"To go where?" Aiken said.

"Victoria Avenue sounds so pleasant," Paris said.

"So, living again on Victoria Avenue," Aiken said, "with just the two of us and our kids?"

"One condition," Paris said. "We absolutely must put together a proper wine cellar, and, Aiken, we should entertain more."

"Sure," Aiken said, "a wine cellar and entertain more."

Mayhem waved a hand back and forth in front of Paris's face. She smiled. Aiken plucked the .303 from Mayhem's hand. "I'll need this," he said.

"Yes, you damn well will," Mayhem said. "I'll see Paris home. You tidy up here, and maybe set out the garbage for collection. There seems to be a lot of garbage here."

"I'll fart around," Aiken said. "I'm gonna unrepress myself just a bit more." He slugged down a few swigs of alcohol and brushed the back of his hand across his lips. When Paris and Mayhem turned the corner out of sight, Aiken zigzagged down the halls. He located the Shift Attendant in the washroom, on the toilet, reading the sports section of the *Free Press* comfortably in a stall. Aiken poked the stall door open. "I'm hunting for the Administrator," Aiken said.

"Whoa," the Shift Attendant said. "Gonna shoot me dead on the toilet? I don't think so."

Aiken pressed the gun barrel against the man's chest. "The Administrator is in Dr. Sam's office," the Shift Attendant said, "congratulating him on the fine job he did on your wife."

Aiken slammed the Shift Attendant in the face with the rifle butt, and the man flipped off the toilet and lay still, messing himself. "Don't be warning anyone," Aiken said, "and make sure you scrub your hands up before you leave. There's germs everywhere."

Aiken trotted down the eighth-floor halls, cradling the rifle and swinging the weapon back and forth, until he arrived at Dr. Sam's office. Inside the office, the Administrator was stretched upright, strapped to Dr. Sam's chair, arms bound with white surgical tape and Dr. Sam's red tie wrapped tightly about his mouth. The Administrator made unintelligible sounds, muffled by the tie.

"This man has no feel for proper therapy," Dr. Sam said. "Something had to be done."

The overhead pipes clanged.

"Sorry about your wife," Dr. Sam said. "Not my idea. But she will now embrace the good life on Victoria Avenue and not argue with you so much. In fact, probably never. But this man—" Dr. Sam rapped the Administrator on the forehead with his knuckles. "This man repressed nothing: a genetic aberration, a mutant! In a crowded elevator he could purposely fart out loud and smile at people in their discomfort."

Aiken nodded. *Another fart theory from Dr. Sam.*

"Always telling me what to do," Dr. Sam said. "I learned Freudian analysis when he was still sucking on his mother's teat."

"Yes," Aiken said, "and now you and I will be taking him down to the shock-therapy room, and you can use the shock gizmo thing on him."

The Administrator emitted grunting noises.

Dr. Sam smiled. "Clearly, Mr. Day, as I reflect upon the situation, the man had no firm grasp of reality, perhaps was sliding into schizophrenia. Yes. Shock treatment is definitely in order."

"Schizophrenia," Aiken said. "Always a bitch." Aiken pinched the cheek of the Administrator. "But also," Aiken said, "after the treatments with the shock gizmo, he may require long-term treatment in the unit."

Dr. Sam smiled again. "Yes, Mr. Day, I understand perfectly: an opportunity to study the long-term effects of shock treatments on a schizophrenic. Good show on you, Mr. Day. Science will be served." Together they hoisted the Administrator into a wheelchair and rolled him down to the lock-down room.

*   *   *

Spittle dribbled down from the Administrator's lip onto his chin. Dr. Sam dabbed a finger to the spit and sucked on the finger, cheeks deflating, then inflating.

"Somewhat acidic," Dr. Sam said. "I'd better make a note of that in his file."

"He's got that persistent tic," Aiken said.

"I'll medicate for that," Dr. Sam said. "We can repress that with enough drugs."

Dr. Sam wiped the spittle from the Administrator's face with the tie. The doctor gestured to the tie. "Gift from my wife," he said. "Be hell to pay if I forget it. She'd be damn upset." He stuffed the tie into his back pocket. Aiken nodded. *Bred into her.*

"The slobbering is to be expected," Dr. Sam said. "He seems to be progressing well, but we have years of work and study ahead of us." A coy smile crossed Dr. Sam's face. "Using what I refer to as *buzz-brain* therapy," Dr. Sam said. ""Buzz-brain,' Mr. Day. I coined that term. Do you like the new terminology?"

"I better get home to my kids," Aiken said.

"Yeah," Dr. Sam said. "Kids are the thing. I'll have the staff lock up old spit face here."

Victoria Avenue

Aiken swung the front screen door open, and the police officer blocking off his porch said, "Mr. Day?"

"Yes."

The officer said, "Mr. Aiken Day?"

"Yes."

The officer yanked him by the shirt and slapped handcuffs on him. He marched Aiken to the idling police car. They drove two blocks down Victoria Avenue, and the officer wrenched the squad car up the driveway of a red-brick home.

"It's two blocks. We might have walked," Aiken said.

"Or I might have hog-tied you and dragged you from the bumper," the officer said.

The officer flipped open the back door of the vehicle, and Aiken climbed out. Aiken hovered on the porch while the officer knocked politely on the front door. Magistrate Frederick sprung the door open. The officer removed the cuffs, and Aiken stepped inside with the judge. A small case of the sweats hit Aiken. The judge began to sweat as well, and then he began to pace: 12 paces up and 12 back. Aiken joined him. *Christ, we're both back in Stalag 8B.*

After several minutes of pacing back and forth, Aiken said, "Why am I here, Stinky?"

"Police officers been nosing about," the Magistrate said, "investigating perhaps, but speaking allegations to me off the record about a ruckus up at the hospital."

"Maybe about my wife?" Aiken said.

Magistrate Frederick nodded. He rose, and Aiken followed toward the back of the house. "Keep with me, please," the Magistrate said. Aiken followed him through the back door and into the yard. "Come meet my dog," Magistrate Frederick said.

A golden Lab, tail wagging, bounced toward Aiken. "What's the dog's name?" Aiken said.

"Justice," said the Magistrate.

Better than Stinky Junior. "Nice touch for a judge," Aiken said. "A dog named Justice."

Magistrate Frederick said, "I promised to bring you to Justice."

"A man should keep his word."

"A man should be a man."

The dog rubbed against Aiken's leg. "Scratch his ears," the Magistrate said. "Of course he'd rather you scratch his balls."

Know the feeling. "Ears are good," Aiken said. Aiken cupped his hand around the dog's ears, scratching behind them.

They stood there a few minutes while Aiken petted the dog. Magistrate Frederick said, "Well, that takes care of that chore."

"Yeah."

The Magistrate headed back to his house, but then he turned and said, "Love to the family, Aiken."

"See you around," Aiken said. *And you too, Stinky Junior.*

*   *   *

The sun dipped low in the sky and slipped toward sunset, sending in the changing early-evening breeze that lifted off the river and floated across the home on Victoria Avenue. The garden showed well, in glorious bloom. Aiken rose from his lawn chair and hovered over the barbecue, feeling the heat blast up. *How many people remember, or even care, that the Germans transported Jew children by rail to the death camps, but thought to reduce the railway fare for those kids by half. Meticulous to a fault, those Germans. Of all the memories floating in my brain, why can't I repress that goddamn memory?* He dropped the first steak onto the grill, watched it sear and smoke, and felt more heat blow up at his face. The sweats were beginning once more.

Adam and Moffat hunched over the picnic table. Rachael sat beside Adam. Adam said, "The president can't stop the war. It's now become about the military-industrial complex."

"I hear you," Moffat said. "It's cool. Everyone understands how industry takes control of the war machine. Take for instance, Kellogg's. The board of directors of Kellogg's helped plan the war, just so they can parachute those tiny boxes of cornflakes to the Indo-Chinese."

Adam laughed. Rachael smiled.

"And the Oreo cookie people," Moffat said. "Even cooler. Those buzzards salivate crazy-like over getting at the Mongolian market." Adam laughed. Rachael smiled.

On the back porch, Honey placed her hand on Paris's arm and whispered something, and they both giggled. An empty wine bottle rested between the two women. The most recent *Vogue* magazine was draped open across Paris's lap. She motioned with her finger to Aiken. "Crank up the barbecue," she said. "A little faster, sweetie."

Aiken wiped a Kleenex against his temple. "Sure thing," he said.

"Daddy," Sarah said. Aiken turned his head, gathered in the wide smile on his daughter, and the heat lessened. She swept over, nestling beside him and putting a hand on his arm. "Daddy," she whispered, "I saw Mr. Johnson and Mrs. Johnson skinny-dipping in their pool last night."

"And both of them in their eighties," Aiken said.

"Honestly, Daddy, you never saw so many wrinkles in your entire life." They remained together, standing quietly.

Paris called over, "Another bottle of wine, please, sweetie."

Sarah wrapped her arm around Aiken's neck and whispered, "I'm telling you, Daddy, I saw them skinny-dipping, and it's going in my essay, wrinkles and all, on how I spent my summer vacation. It will blow this town wide open." She shook her head. "And I am going to sell the story to *Reader's Digest*."

Aiken smiled.

"Another bottle of white, sweetie," Paris said.

* * *

Aiken pulled on his pajama bottoms, checked his forehead with a hidden motion, and found it dry. Paris rested in the bedroom chair, fussing with her nails. "Aiken dear, please help me," she said. She stuck out both hands.

"You've painted your nails," Aiken said.

"But each hand is coloured in different shades," she said. "Choose the most attractive."

"What?" Aiken said.

She stamped her foot. "Choose the colour, Aiken."

Aiken stepped across the room, took her hands, and squinted. *The same damn colour on each hand—so maybe a trick question, or maybe not.*

Paris waited. Aiken pointed to a hand. "This one."

"This will become my signature colour, then," Paris said. She dabbed remover on the other hand and said, "I'm so pleased to have that chore out of the way."

"Why don't I fetch some wine," Aiken said. "Maybe a touch of wine, before we cuddle up?"

"My nails will need time to dry, sweetie. Finishing touches make a woman desirable. Maybe we could do it tomorrow night." Aiken nodded. *Pencil me in.*

"But I'll have to check my horoscope," she said.

So maybe pencil me out? This is not the feisty woman I fell in love with and married. Would I rather have that one back, instead of the one who keeps the latest Vogue at her bedside?

Aiken slid the gold band off his finger. After a few seconds, he kissed it and slid it back on his finger. *Love will out.*

He removed his pajama bottoms, wrapped himself in a housecoat, and left the bedroom. He traipsed down the stairs, past the main floor, and down into the basement. There he scrounged about in the storage room among the paint cans and discovered a spray can. He read the label. "Brilliant Electric Blue," he said. "Perfect." Opening the housecoat and gritting his teeth, he sprayed his private parts with the bright blue paint and, after a few minutes, wrapped himself up in the housecoat again. *A man does what a man has to do.*

In the kitchen, he opened a bottle of red—a medium-priced Bordeaux—and hooked two glasses. *Goddamn, but this itches like hell. I'll need to sandpaper this shit off.*

Upstairs, he entered the bedroom and set the wine bottle and glasses on the dresser. Paris was in silk lounging pajamas, her head lying on the pillow, flipping through the pages of *Vogue Magazine*.

Aiken poured wine into the two glasses and sipped from one. "I'm feeling blue, sweetie."

She smiled, fingering the magazine. "Not tonight, dear, remember—the nails."

"It's getting damn serious," Aiken said. "I'm really feeling blue." He flipped the gown wide open, holding it open until she glanced down at him. She laughed so hard that she actually fell on the floor.

In the morning, he rinsed the two wineglasses in the kitchen sink and tossed the empty bottle. The house felt empty without Paris. *Out civil-rightsing again.* He reached down and scratched again. *Goddamn, it is gonna take sandpaper. Or maybe a damn blowtorch.*

Psych Ward, Windsor Hospital

The newscaster on TV said, "The 82nd and 101st Airborne units have regained control of Detroit." He paused before continuing, peering down at his notes. "But a strong sense of moral outrage lingers among the city's white community. Why Detroit, in 1967? Why not Birmingham? Racism is clearly much worse in Birmingham." The announcer smiled; his white teeth glittered. "We now take you back to our regularly featured program."

The TV returned to "I Love Lucy."

"And about goddamn time," the Fat Man said. People nodded.

Victoria Avenue

The black Lab stretched out in the grass, twisting his head to look up at Aiken. "It's you and me, bud," Aiken said. The dog made no reply. Aiken drank beer from a green bottle. He pissed in the flower bed while staring up at the star-spattered night sky. "Nothing like pissing in a flower bed," he said. The dog farted. *No repression around here.*

About the Author

Allan (Dare) Pearce ("Dare" to his family, friends, and colleagues) practises law in Windsor, Ontario, with the law firm *Pearce, Ducharme Family Law*. This is the second novel Mr. Pearce has authored about his hero Aiken Day.